ABOVE THE FAT

THOMAS CHADWICK grew up in Wiltshire and now splits his time between London and Ghent. His stories have been shortlisted for the *White Review* prize, the *Ambit* prize, and the Bridport prize, and longlisted for the Galley Beggar prize. He is an editor of *Hotel* magazine.

First published in paperback in 2019 by Splice,
48 Milner Road, Birmingham B29 7RQ.

The right of Thomas Chadwick to be identified as the author of
this work has been asserted in accordance with
Section 77 of the Copyright, Designs and Patents Act 1988.

Paperback Edition: ISBN 978-1-9999741-7-6
Ebook Edition: ISBN 978-1-9999741-8-3

Cover Design: Wirat Suandee and
Jasmina Putnik/Shutterstock.

ABOVE THE FAT

Thomas Chadwick

ThisIsSplice.co.uk

Contents

The answers to all the questions that beset you are not in facts,
which are the greatest illusion of all, but in your own heart,
in your own habits, in your limitations,
in your fear.

Hilary Mantel
Eight Months on Ghazzah Street

O ye hypocrites, ye can discern the face of the sky;
but can ye not discern the signs of the times?

Matthew 16:3

A train passes through
the Ruhr region
in the early morning

TURNED SOIL that glows cobalt in light. Blue skies crossed with cirrus and jets. The sound of snoring. The hum of air conditioning. Brakes. Rails on embankments that look down at houses. Lights turning on in cold kitchens. Fractions of moon. Walls painted white. Trees without leaves. Ivy. Moss. Birch. Old ladies pulling on their cigarettes and waving to the train from a concrete balcony. The gravel of unannounced stations. Firs that hang greedily onto their leaves. Overhead cables. Parallel tracks. The *Hbf* that in full German reads Hauptbahnhof and which somehow almost sounds like a station. Shoulders that hunch. Anoraks. Cagoules. Coats. Hoods. Gloves. Scarves. Wool. The LEDs that allow doors to open. The iron pillars decorated with rivets and rust. The murmur of stomachs. Windows shadowed with dust. Hands caught in pockets. Feet caught in steps. Straps caught in doors. Eyes caught by light. Light that is blue. More birch. Grass that is brown or worn. Churches that are old or simply spired or complex or no longer used for worship. Cars without headlights. Buses with billboards. Fields that are furrowed. Platforms that fold. Nests hung in trees. The still, standing water beneath the limbs of willow. Places with moss. The persistence of advertising. The creak of seats. Vents. Roads. More firs. Rock. Lines of light. The really huge amount of metal. Pillars. Rails.

Wires. Fences. Cars. Signals. Plugs. Crash barriers. Windows. Instructions for emergencies. Hills. Mounds. Rises. Slopes. Peaks. Hollows. Valleys. Holes. Places to hide. Gable ends. Gardens. Livestock. Dogs. Frames for greenhouses that have yet to be built. Long ruined castles. The remnants of crops. The occasional flag. Chimneys. Power stations. Warehouses. Goods in. Birds. The hum of fossil fuel. Advertisements for wood. The slopes of hillsides. The tin roofs of barns. Cars at junctions. Windmills. Lakes. Thickets. So much birch it's untrue. Pitches for sports. Allotments. Water towers. Municipal buildings. The drays of squirrels. The rocking of rails. Solar panels. Motorways. Multiple carriageways. Quarries. Just a totally implausible amount of birch. Mounds of mud. The growth of grass. The persistence of concrete. The humility of brick. The half-finished roofs of partially built homes. Rivers.

Birch

1997

BUSINESS BOOMED. Optimism was shooting up everywhere and bursting into flower. Music was jocular. Sport was effusive. Soon it would be possible to do the most wonderful things with computers. People woke and felt buoyant. Cereal was measured out with glee. Steam lifted from the mugs of recently reconciled marriages. Parents treated children to extravagant lunch box items. People would turn to their loved ones and say things like, "I can't wait to read the paper" and "What a time to be alive." But the people had been caught out before. They knew from history books and the Bible and *Panorama* that no flower can last forever; they knew that after summer the petals fold and fail, the leaves whither, the plant dies. The people knew that in good times smart people put down roots. So the people built houses.

People were building a whole lot of houses. To build houses you need timber and because Stuart's business traded solely in timber the optimism soon wormed its way into the wood at Ford's Mill. Orders were rampant. Builders bought four-by-two by the pack and skirting board by the bundle. Stuart sent his lorries out full every morning and watched them return empty by lunch. Often they would be sent out again because of all the fucking optimism about all the fucking houses; because business was booming and everyone was having such a great time; because it was all so serenely upbeat. "Education, education, education," said New Labour. Smart people build houses.

Stuart was smart. Too smart to sell timber for a living, people said. Far too smart. Could have been a lawyer, they said. Could have been a damn fine lawyer. A teacher at Stuart's school—Mr. Charters—had been certain that Stuart had it in him to be a damn fine lawyer.

"You should go to university," he told Stuart, "and study law."

"Dad wants me to join the family business."

"What business is that?"

"The timber business."

Everyone thought Stuart was making a huge mistake turning down the opportunity to be such a damn fine lawyer. "I never even got into law school," he protested. Such a waste, they said. Stuart's loyalties were at home. That was his problem. His loyalties. He was too damn loyal by half.

That spring, with optimism accumulating along rivers like froth, the foreman, Ted Coles, turned to Stuart and said he'd never seen the like. Ford's Mill was an old-fashioned merchant, which meant it moved goods. The business bought timber in large volumes and sold it in smaller volumes. With the change in volume came a change in price. The change in price was the profit. Because the volumes were variable, so too was the difference in price and so too was the profit. The more timber they bought the cheaper the cost. The more they sold the more money they made. "It's economies of scale," Stuart's Dad always said. To Stuart it was just common sense.

For years Ford's Mill had been run by Stuart's old man and his faith in economies of scale. Roughly a year after Stuart left school and started working for his Dad a competitor tried to buy them out. Representatives from Watt's Timber Ltd. arrived in smart cars and pulled documents from a briefcase that said that if Stuart's Dad gave them Ford's Mill they would give him just shy of one million pounds. It was a substantial offer, the member of the acquisitions team explained, for the rights to the business and assets. Stuart's Dad called Stuart into his wood-panelled office, with the oak table and plaque for Timber Merchant of the Year (Western Division) from 1986.

"I'm retiring," he said. "This is as much your decision as mine."

Stuart looked at the numbers and tried to picture what that much money would mean. "It's just a few sheds and some timber? What do they know that we don't?"

His Dad smiled. "That's exactly what I was thinking."

A few years later business burst into fucking flames.

By the summer of '97, Stuart was buying obscene volumes of timber. Everyone agreed that currently the best timber was coming out of Sweden. At industry events Stuart would watch people lean across tables and say things like, "There's some damn fine timber coming out of Sweden." Stuart might have agreed but strictly speaking he had no say whether the timber at Ford's Mill came from Sweden or Norway or anywhere else. Instead Stuart bought it from two wholesalers: one based in Hull, the other at Shoreham. His Dad had traded with Mitchall's at Hull and Jennings' at Shoreham since the '70s. They did good deals. They were loyal. They were a far better bet than Peter's at Harwich and Bamber's at Portsmouth. Stuart's old man knew Mr. Jennings and Mr. Mitchall personally and when Stuart started out in the industry he was introduced. Soon he, too, came to trust them. When his Dad died both firms sent flowers.

Construction is seasonal. Normally trade slows down in autumn and all but stops in winter. In '97 no-one slowed down. Instead people saw a chance to get ahead. People were giddy with excitement and so said things like, "Fuck the frost let's carry on building." They hired heaters and lamps and kept at it. Stuart was getting through more wood than ever. Timber arrived on the racks in the morning and was out for delivery by lunch. He had to take someone on in the office to help Carol keep on top of the orders. Craig was fresh from Sixth Form. He wore glasses and was full of ideas.

"You should get computers," he said.

Stuart laughed.

"I'm serious. They'd save time and paperwork."

"We sell timber. Buy for a dollar, sell for a pound. We're not putting men on the moon," Stuart said.

Computers or no computers business persisted. Profits were large. Stuart's wife planned a new kitchen. "Your Dad would have been so proud," she said at breakfast, while eating their extravagant cereal.

I could have been a damn fine lawyer, thought Stuart.

The orders to Hull and Shoreham were non-stop. Both Mitchall and Jennings rang Stuart personally to tell him they'd never seen the like. "The way business is," Jennings added. "You might as well take the whole boat."

Really, thought Stuart, the whole boat.

That morning when the lorries were out for delivery, Stuart sat in the wood-panelled office at his Dad's old oak desk and thought about what Jennings had said. He did some sums. He logged some costs. He asked himself how much of what he paid to Jennings found its way across the water to Sweden and how much stayed put in Shoreham. He wondered whether a smart person—someone who, say, might have been a damn fine lawyer had things been different—might make a different negotiation when business was this fucking good?

They've always done good deals out of Shoreham, he heard his Dad say.

But how do you know for sure when you've never tried to get better?

They're good people. They're loyal. That still counts for a lot in this business. We should stick with them. It's common sense.

"It's economies of fucking scale," Stuart said.

Stuart asked around. He found a mill in Sweden that might deal direct. Not the biggest mill, but a moderate one with ambitions to grow. Everyone knows that business is all about growth. Stuart made the call from home, sat on their new bed, with the phone resting on the Egyptian cotton his wife had so thoughtfully picked out. The first time the phone rang the continental bleat vibrated inside Stuart's skull and he thought he was going to be sick. The second time, someone picked up.

"Hello," Stuart said.

"Ah, England," she said.

Her name was Emma and it was possible. It was all possible. In fact Stuart should have been in touch a long time ago.

"Who do you deal with in Shoreham?"

"Jennings."

"Well, Jennings has been—how do you say it in English?— *ripping you off.*"

Emma's voice was fresh and warm and promising. She sounded like raindrops on new tiles; bare feet on warm gravel; a new wind through old leaves.

"Do you have a fax machine?" Stuart asked.

"We prefer email," she said.

Stuart bought a computer. He placed an order. Timber arrived. The quality was high. The price was low. Housebuilders purred. New customers came. Fresh deals were struck. Beautiful lengths of timber passed through the gates at Ford's Mill. Stuart would go out to touch them; to run a hand along their grain; to press his face against a knot and inhale the scent.

A letter arrived from Hull asking if everything was okay. Mr. Mitchall had noticed that Stuart had stopped placing orders. He knew that winter could be a tough time, but because of their strong relationship he would do anything he could to help out. As it happened, he'd been looking at Stuart's terms on some core products and had decided that they could do better. Stuart rolled the letter into a ball and hurled it at the wall. The next day he did the same to a letter from Shoreham.

Stuart sat at the computer now installed on his father's oak desk. His hands smelt pleasantly of pine as he tapped away at an email. Computers turned out to be easy. People made altogether too much fuss. But then Stuart was smart—a damn fine lawyer were it not for family loyalties. He finished the email and brushed the sawdust from his shirt sleeves. He hit SEND. It was all common sense with computers.

He thought often of Emma. They spoke from time to time on the phone. Stuart liked to hear the promise in her voice and the echo in her vowels. He wondered if she smelled like her timber. Once he asked her to describe the view from her window. She talked of sparse grass and tall trees, men in plaid shirts and hard hats.

"Can I come and visit?" Stuart said suddenly.

"The sawmill?"

"Yes. I'd like to see where the timber comes from, where the trees grow."

"Yes, you should visit. But don't come now. It's winter. Everything is covered in snow. All I will be able to show you are things underneath snow and a mill where it gets dark before three. You will bring an insubstantial jacket. You might freeze to death. You will miss your wife. Come in spring."

"How did you know I was married?"

"I do now," she said.

1998

THAT SPRING BUSINESS EXPLODED. Wood was omniscient. Stuart could not get enough of it. He took on more staff. He bought two new lorries. He did a deal on some land with the neighbouring farmer and got planning permission to build a new warehouse. In April he flew out of Bristol. The sky was clear and the plane skidded down over pines, the trees densely packed along either side of the runway. In Stockholm his hotel was in Södermalm. On the first day he admired the Opera House and the park and the quayside. He visited a museum about coins. It grew cold. He bought a new coat. He ate cinnamon buns and drank coffee. He tried pickled fish and licked his lips. On the second day he took a boat trip out to the islands and marvelled at the clean lines of the landscape. He found a small cove and stood by the tide with the water lapping at his feet. On the third day he took a train.

Borlänge was only recently defrosted. Everything was made of wood and surrounded by trees. At the hotel Stuart was encouraged to sauna. He walked into a room of steam. He sat alone and sweated profusely. He thought of Emma. He felt light-headed. He was joined by a German businessman.

"I'm Dietmar, you must be here for the timber?" he said.

Dietmar discarded his towel. Through the steam, Stuart nodded.

"What's timber doing in Germany?" he asked, in an attempt at conversation.

"Booming probably," said Dietmar. "But I'm in paper so really I wouldn't know."

"Oh," said Stuart. "What's paper doing?"

"Paper is going fucking insane."

Emma called the hotel to check that Stuart had found it. Her voice arrived dusted with nutmeg. She said the hotel would want Stuart to sauna. He told her he already had. She laughed. Stuart felt the receiver warm slightly against his check.

"Do you have dinner plans?" she asked.

"Not yet."

"You will," she said.

Stuart sat in the lobby until Dietmar convinced him to walk into town.

"But I have dinner plans."

"It's early," Dietmar said. "We should go and look round."

Dietmar was insistent. He was also angry. He had got into the paper trade at just the right time and he hated himself. "They are paying me so damn much," he explained. "Even if I wanted to leave, I couldn't. No-one can turn down the amount of money they are paying me. It's criminal."

"How much are they paying you?"

"So much, look there's a bar."

Dietmar insisted that they enter the bar. The only other customer was an old man in snow shoes. Over expensive drinks that he insisted on paying for, Dietmar explained that he wasn't meant to be working in paper. He was meant to be a political journalist. "I come from a long line of devoted reporters. I studied at the Freie Universität in Berlin, I interned at *Handelsblatt*. But news was slow. I ended up in paper. I'm a huge disappointment to my family. They tell this joke at Christmas, I will try to translate: *You were meant to be in the paper not in paper.*"

Dietmar laughed hard across the empty bar. Stuart took a sip from his expensive beer.

"It's not funny is it?" said Dietmar. "We should drink snaps?"

They drank snaps. Two of them, in quick succession. Stuart felt groggy. Dietmar enquired about a titty bar that had been recommended by a sales rep from Austria.

"That's not really my thing," Stuart said.

"My father spent four years as an undercover reporter. He exposed racism towards the Turkish community and the exploitation of steel workers. I am reduced to looking at Swedish tits before I visit a saw mill. My life is very sad. What were you meant to do with your life?"

"People used to say I'd make a good lawyer."

"See. Our lives are tragic. My father was a wanted man for a time. He was given a medal last year for his vigilance. Let me buy you more snaps."

They drank more snaps. The old man shuffled off in his snow shoes. The barman returned to say that there was no titty bar in Borlänge.

"This is bullshit," Dietmar said. "Never trust a competitor."

They left. Stuart tried to go back to the hotel, Dietmar said they couldn't quit now: "Sometimes in the nice bars they lie about the nasty ones," he said. They found a bar that advertised a Rage Against the Machine concert in Karlstad. Inside were several large Swedish men sat beneath beards and biker jackets and two very tall girls with blonde hair and leather trousers. Guns N' Roses was playing on repeat. There was no snaps. Dietmar bought beers.

"I hate my job," he explained. "It's the least I can do."

He tried to speak to the girls but they just laughed and said they were leaving. He asked the bearded Swedes about the titty bar he'd been told about by the sales rep from Austria. The Swedes just laughed.

"Are you here for the timber?" they asked.

"Yes, we're here for the timber."

They nodded. They said that they worked in the forest.

"What do you do there?" Stuart asked.

They laughed again and said they cut down trees. Stuart wanted very much to leave. Dietmar bought everyone drinks. "They pay me so goddamn much," he said. "What do they expect?" At midnight Dietmar ordered a cab from which he stumbled to his room. The concierge stopped Stuart to say that someone called Emma had come by around seven. She had left a message to say that she was sorry to miss him and was looking forward to meeting him tomorrow.

Out loud, in the wood-panelled reception, Stuart swore. He drank water. He cleaned his teeth. He cursed. He decided it was not possible to call his wife. From the window of his room he could see a small hill where pine trees stood in silhouette against a moonlit sky.

Emma was tall and so blonde her hair was almost white. It glinted like frost as she shook Stuart's hand in the lobby. She smiled and said nothing about dinner. Stuart was deeply in love.

"I see you met Dietmar," she said.

She drove them out of the small town and into the trees. They drove through trees, past trees, around trees. Along one stretch of road the trees were so dense that you could not tell where one ended and the next began.

"I feel terrible," said Dietmar from the backseat.

The sawmill was in a clearing. Emma worked in a wide-windowed office on the first floor where she offered them coffee. Dietmar drank his black with biscuits. From the window you could see sparse grass and tall trees, men in plaid shirts and hard hats. At a lightwood table Emma gave a short history of the mill.

It was founded by her grandfather in 1933. It grew rapidly after the Second World War and very soon established itself as an exporter to Europe. Her father took over in the '70s and managed the mill until '95 when Emma and her brother took over. Dietmar said it was a beautiful story and he needed more coffee. Emma pressed on with the tour.

Stuart met people. Swedish people with fair hair and broad smiles. He was given a hard hat and ear plugs and led into an enormous sawmill. He watched a tree arrive whole with its bark still on and leave in roughly sawn planks. Dietmar disappeared to the bathroom and then returned to bellow out questions about provenance. Stuart watched Emma's hand as she led them out of the mill to the forest where trees would be ready in forty years' time.

Stuart inhaled the scent of the forest, his bare face taut in the sunlight. Emma had changed into boots to show them the trees. Dietmar asked about lunch. He repeated that he hated his job and made further reference to how much he got paid. Emma walked through the pines, down a narrow path until the canopy disappeared and they were surrounded by birch. The trees were young, saplings, barely ten feet tall. Their bark peeled slightly from their trunks, branches shot out of clefts in their stems and up above the new leaves blushed pink in the morning sun.

"Do you have a canteen here?" Dietmar asked.

"You should pay attention," Emma said. "We're growing the birch especially for you."

Dietmar said he was too cold and stomped his way back to the office.

"I called by the hotel," Emma said.

Stuart stared into the silver branches. "Dietmar made me go drinking." He stopped. "What did you mean you're growing them specially for him?"

When a tree is cut for timber, it is divided into three separate products. The lower, central timber is the oldest and densest wood and thus of the highest quality. It is milled and planed and used for joinery and structural beams. The middle section, leading up to the branches, is used for carcassing and more general construction, lengths of 4x2, 6x2, 8x2 and so on. It is bundled into packs and sold to housebuilders. Everything else from the bark to the branches and twigs at the top is given over to paper and pulp. Some of it is ground up into sawdust or shavings and mixed with glue to make MDF or Stirling board, but most of it is used for paper. In Borlänge the separation of the products occurred in the sawmill. It was a seamless process. The lengths of timber were stacked on racks indoors awaiting delivery while the paper and pulp were bundled up and sold to people like Dietmar. He had only really come to see a byproduct. Maybe that was why he was angry.

"Dietmar is a huge problem," Emma said as they walked through the birch. "Him and people like him keep demanding pulp. But the paper is not why we grow the trees. It takes over thirty years for a pine tree to reach a decent height, fifty for it to reach maturity. We can't just cut them all down for paper. It's unsustainable. So two years ago I planted this birch. It's a new idea. My father thinks I am mad. A whole section of woodland devoted to birch! But others are doing it too. Birch is fast growing. In ten years it will be ready and we can chop it all down and turn it into paper."

They were deep into the forest now, with birch as far as the eye could see; young limbs blistered in the late morning light.

"Besides," said Emma. "They're kind of pretty, don't you think?"

"They're beautiful," Stuart said.

Back home Stuart made changes. He hired a sales team to ease the pressure on Carol and bought an integrated computer system that covered purchasing, sales, delivery, and stock. Craig was promoted to systems administrator and given his own office. He purred with delight. Only Carol remained unconvinced. "It cuts down paperwork," Stuart said in a bid to persuade her.

But this was a lie. It did not.

Every time anything was done on a computer a printer leapt into action. There were four of them at Ford's Mill: one in the sales office, one in the purchasing office, one in the yard office, one in Stuart's office. They fizzed constantly throughout the day, churning out reams of paper framed by dotted edges that people ripped off and left scattered across the floor like confetti. The paper was carbonless copy paper that produced three identical sheets. This meant that the information could be divided between the office, the yard, and the customer. It also meant that every time anyone

printed anything, whenever printers jammed or incorrect information was sent, the waste tripled.

The printers jammed all the time. Craig would be summoned
to hunch over the ribbon and tease out the offending sheets. The
waste went in the bin. The excess sheets went in the bin. Every
day someone went round the office picking up the frayed edges
and putting them in the bin. Sometimes, often when Stuart was
least expecting it, the printer in his office would start spewing out
paper for no reason—that paper also went in the bin.

Every week—sometimes twice a week—Stuart emailed Emma
an order. He pictured her computer leaping into action by the
window that looked out over the mill. He imagined her taking
breaks during lunchtime and walking out through the thick snow,
to stand in the midst of the birch. He remembered the way her
hands moved as she explained about paper and pulp. He tried to
think of things to add at the end of his emails: How's your family?
How's your father? How's your birch?

"Birch is good," Emma wrote. "It is growing well. We hope to
harvest in eight years, not ten, which is good because right now
the paper mills are really squeezing production."

Stuart had bought all the land between Ford's Mill and the
main road to make way for new racks of timber. The farmer who
sold it to him also offered him the acres on the far side that led
back towards the canal. It was just a field and a small copse
where he would rear pheasants for city bankers to take the train
down from London and shoot. It was not a large bit of land, but it
was Stuart's if he wanted it. Stuart decided he did.

In an email to Emma he sketched out his plan. He could fit
several hundred trees into the acreage and in England, where the
growing season was longer, they could be ready in just eight years'
time. "Dear Emma," he wrote, "I'm getting into the birch game!"

Emma replied instantly. She was excited. They could compare notes. If Stuart's grew quicker she would be jealous. Stuart smiled. His printer began spewing out paper.

"Are you building more sheds?" his wife asked later that evening.

"I'm going to plant birch trees."

"Birch?"

"They use it to make paper."

"Paper?"

She was confused. Stuart left the new extension before she could ask what his father would say or whether he'd thought it all though. Besides, he *had* thought it through. Paper was everywhere. With computers and emails and the web there was more printing than ever. Everyone was drowning in the stuff. And it was his mill now, not his father's. He was making changes. He was shaking things up. Every generation had to betray the traditions of the previous one. That was common sense. And thus the birch, well, that was economies of scale. Yes, he'd thought it all through. Stuart was smart, remember; an almost lawyer, remember; and smart people made changes. They did not stand still.

"Paper?" his wife repeated later in bed.

Stuart rolled over.

"Isn't everything going to be done by computers? Please be careful."

"Careful of what?" Stuart cried.

His wife cowered behind the Egyptian cotton and muttered that they should think of the future. At one point she tried to take his hand. He threw it away and slept downstairs. The next morning a letter arrived from Shoreham to say that Mr. Jennings was dead.

"You should send flowers," Stuart's wife said.

The birch saplings arrived before Christmas when the ground was cracking with frost. There were hundreds of them. Small stems of silver wrapped in hessian. Five men came to do the planting. Stuart stayed to watch. Holes were dug. Trees were raised. Earth was moved. Roots were covered. By four o'clock everyone had left and Stuart was able to wander through the new trees as the sun set around them. The ground was compacted from where lorries had driven and people had stood. The trees were spread a few meters apart. Barely five feet tall. In ten years they'd be ready to harvest. "I thought you bought that land for a warehouse?" Carol asked from an office that was knee deep in paper. Stuart ignored the question and locked his door. Triplicate copies were piling up across the floor. He clambered over them until he reached the window and could look across the yard, through the street lamps that guarded the forklifts, towards the silhouettes of the birch.

Every morning Stuart walked across the timber yard and through the wide gate that separated the mill from the birch. He let Ted Coles take care of deliveries and spent time amidst his new trees. He felt their young branches. He ran his fingers over their blistering skin, felt shreds of bark muddy his fingertips. He wondered in what direction the new shoots would burst and whether there would be pink leaves next spring. A few of the trees did not take and died where they sat in the soil. Tears ran down Stuart's face as he removed the branches and burnt them. He buried the roots where they lay. In the evenings he would sit on the thin grass that grew up beneath the trees and listen to the sound of the wind. His wife was pregnant now. The baby was due in June.

That May, Stuart received a complaint. A phone call was put through to his office from a man called Keith. Keith was head of purchasing at a big housebuilding firm in the west. He said he would have to be blunt.

"The timber you've been sending has been a load of crap. The wood's all wet and warped and the quality is low."

Stuart apologised. It was an oversight. A mistake. There would be a full refund and the promise never to do so again. Stuart would see to it personally that this was never repeated.

"I appreciate that," said Keith.

Printers leapt to work to correct the oversight. Emergency deliveries were made. A week later another complaint arrived from a man named Mark. Then from Joe. Then Steven.

"It's Sweden," Ted Coles explained. "They're sending us lousy wood."

Stuart shook his head. That night he sat for a long time amidst the birch. He listened to rooks crowing as they came in to roost along the canal, cawing at one another as they negotiated their perches. It was dark by the time he got home.

After three weeks of complaints, Stuart called Emma.

"Stuart! How's your birch?"

"Beautiful, how is yours?"

"Slow. Far too slow."

Stuart explained about the problems with quality. Emma apologised. It was the paper, she said. Between friends, it was all because of the fucking paper. Orders were off the scale. They had harvested too many trees the year before. More trees than they could fit in their sheds. Some of the wood had been stood outside over winter beneath tarpaulins. "We invested in the very best tarpaulin," Emma explained, "but the very best tarpaulin is no match for Swedish snow." Anyway, this was beside the point. Stuart should not have been sold the timber left outside. As a valued customer, as a friend, he should have been sold the timber from indoors. Emma apologised. It was an oversight. A mistake. There would be a full refund and the promise never to do so again. Emma would see to it personally that this was never repeated.

"Anyway," she said, "I hear congratulations are in order."

The next load of timber that arrived at Ford's Mill was the worst Ted Coles had ever seen. He sent it all back and sulked in the delivery office. Emma was not in when Stuart rang. A sales clerk cut the price on the phone. Stuart cut his prices. Printers whirred. Keith emailed to say that he was switching suppliers. Mark said the same. Most people just stopped placing orders. Timber stood still on racks. Piles of grey wood lay propped up in mounds, beside the paper that Stuart did not know how to recycle. The baby was due in a month. The birch was seven feet tall.

Shortly before his son was born, Stuart rang Shoreham.

"I was sorry to hear about your old man, I have this horrible feeling I forgot to send flowers."

"My old man?"

"Your father, Mr. Jennings?"

"You've got the wrong bloke. Bob Jennings' son sold up first chance he could. We're owned by Peter's & Bamber's now."

The sales manager, whose name Stuart missed, was sympathetic. He listened attentively. He knew about all the problems in Sweden. It wasn't just Sweden, though. Everywhere had harvested their forests to keep up with the paper. "There are stacks of timber slowly rotting across the whole of northern Europe," the sales manager said. It was a struggle for quality all round, but Stuart was lucky he'd called when he did. "There's a lot of clout up here after the merger. We've been able to squeeze the mills to get the good stock, but it comes at a price."

Stuart was quoted a figure that was almost double what he'd been paying Emma at Borlänge. In truth there was no real choice. It did not matter that the timber was good. Responses were blunt. Phones were placed on receivers. Memories were short. Sales fell. Printers jammed. Wood wasted away on the racks. Stuart's son screamed all night and in the day the forklifts lay silent. Craig left to take a job in IT. Carol retired. Ted Coles said he'd never

seen the like. The paper was taken away by the council in a lorry
that cost Stuart four hundred pounds. The birch reached shoulder
height. Stuart spent whole days there now, walking through the
trees, touching them, caressing their leaves, wondering if he would
ever have the heart to fell them.

1999

BUSINESS SLOWED. Business stalled. Business fell off a fucking cliff.
The delegation from Watts' Timber—which included two directors,
the regional operations director, and, in order to try and push it
all through that same day, the Chairman, Peter Watts, himself—
stepped out of Stuart's wood-panelled office and examined the
site at Ford's Mill. Watts' Timber had been hit by the slump, just
like everyone else, but Mr. Watts knew that only those operations
that stood still would flounder. As soon as signs of a downturn
were felt he set about buying up those sites and businesses that
blocked the stability of his market share. Often, as was the case
with Ford's Mill, Mr. Watts had tried to buy these sites and
businesses before. Mr. Watts had always been surprised that old
Mr. Ford would not give in, but he'd assumed that Stuart would
have no interest in timber.

Unlike many of the sites Mr. Watts had purchased that week,
where the businesses would be dismantled and the land sold on
at a profit, Ford's Mill was, in fact, an enviable location. Stuart,
who sat mute in the office as his lawyer examined the paperwork,
had acted prudently in the intervening decade. He had bought
more land and had planning permission approved to build a new
warehouse. There were good staff by all accounts and an integrated computer system, which would allow Stuart's stock to become
Mr. Watts' stock with nothing but the click of a button. Yet despite
all these changes, Mr. Watts did not need to see an account ledger
to know that all was not well. A business that grew this fast could

not hope to survive unless it put down some roots. As soon as Mr. Watts got word that Ford's Mill was struggling—through Peter's & Bamber's, as it turned out—he got his acquisitions team to start work on an offer. At first Stuart refused, just as his father had refused ten years earlier. Mr. Watts listened. He took note of the expansion and the extra sheds. He increased his price. Stuart wavered. The price was increased one final time and Mr. Watts was driven down to Ford's Mill to sign the paperwork in person. He did not mind the excursion. He liked buying things and he had an aunt who lived nearby who was old and who he intended to visit. He would drop in after he'd inspected the mill and enjoy a cup of tea. It was important to take time for one's family. Peter Watts said as much to Stuart earlier in the office where old Mr. Ford had once refused to sell the business but where Stuart was now only too glad.

"I understand you have a young son," Peter Watts said.

Stuart said nothing and stared at the wall.

The delegation walked past the timber sheds towards the outdoor racks where the forklifts and summer rain had turned the ground into mud. Ever astute, Mr. Watts caught sight of the gate that led through to the birch trees in the adjacent lot.

"Do we know who owns that?"

"It belongs to the mill."

Peter Watts sounded surprised. "Some conservation project, I suppose. It's good land. We can use it."

"Actually," said the man from the acquisitions team, "it still belongs to the mill."

"Why do we not own it?"

"He refused to sell. We offered more money, but he wouldn't listen. It's only a few trees. It's worth nothing on its own. I'm not even sure what they are."

"We couldn't figure out why he hadn't built more sheds," another member of the acquisitions team said. "There's planning permission and with the amount of timber that's been left out in the open it would have made far more sense to build cover."

Peter Watts snarled as Stuart emerged from the office and made his way across the yard. He did not look towards the group of men in suits. Instead he walked right past them, lifting his legs through the stolid mud in the direction of the gate. When he reached it he lifted his leg onto the bar and vaulted onto the other side. Without breaking stride he continued walking, through the birch trees, past the silver skins that grew so swiftly in the sweet Stanton silt, until at some point the blushing leaves enveloped him and he disappeared from sight.

And the Glass
Cold Against His Face

AT 6.34AM THE SCAFFOLDING PLATFORM, from which Simon McNiven was cleaning windows, collapsed. Somehow, in the same instant that the lightweight aluminium platform fell from beneath his feet—taking his rags, bucket, squeegee, and lunchbox hurtling down the glass front of the eighty-five-storey building—Simon managed to force his hands into the 4cm crack in the glass that marked the threshold between the 79th and 80th floors. Quite how he did this Simon did not know but at the same moment as the aluminium frame crunched into the pavement below, Simon found himself hanging from the 80th floor with his arms stretching out above his head in the early morning sun.

There appeared to be two possible outcomes: either someone down there was going to spot Simon up here and arrange for him to be rescued before his fingers grew tired and slipped, or Simon was going to fall to his death on the pavement. Glancing at his wristwatch, which sat just below the fingers taut inside the crack, 6.34am struck Simon as a little early. Anything after 8.00am would offer a far better chance of being seen, and even 7.30am would be okay, but at this time of morning the number of people walking along the pavement below the building would be slim. For reasons that Simon did not want to think about right now, his phone was left sitting on the kitchen table at his home.

Simon's arms were already beginning to feel the strain. He was a fit and healthy man—twenty-nine years old, no medical history to speak of and athletic in build. It often seemed to Simon that he was a good deal more athletic than his job demanded, yet hanging from a small crack between two enormous panes of glass seemed to be causing his arms to tremble and his fingers to grow a little red towards the tips. The possibility of Simon manoeuvring himself to someplace where he might be a little more comfortable did not look good. For a start, Simon's fingers and arms were straining so much that he did not dare release the pressure of one grip to shuffle across, lest it place so much pressure on the other grip that he would be forced to let go entirely. On top of that, Simon knew from cleaning the windows up there that the crack in the glass simply wrapped around the building like a belt, only meeting another crack that ran down the building's spine at the corners.

Simon swore loudly.

"Isn't it," a voice replied.

Very slowly, mindful not to disturb the the tension between his arms and fingers, and noting that his watch now read 6.35am, Simon turned his head to look along the width of the building.

"Hi," said the voice.

There, perhaps ten or fifteen metres away from Simon, hanging from the same crack in the glass, was another man.

"How lucky are we?" said the man.

Given that until a minute ago Simon had been separated from the 80-floor drop by a scaffolding platform which had somehow unbuckled or fractured to leave him hanging from his fingertips, Simon didn't really feel lucky.

"Would you call this lucky?" he said.

"Think about it, what are the chances of both of us being up here today, and both of us managing to grab onto this crack when the scaffold fell?"

It struck Simon that had this man not been so *lucky*, as he put it, and fallen down with the scaffolding, the chances of Simon being spotted up here would have been significantly higher. It was still possible, of course, that someone would come across the buckled aluminium platform on the street below, look up and figure out what was going on, but there were huge amounts of building work going on in the area and the pavements were regularly obstructed. Simon could picture pedestrians stepping politely around the platform in a way that seemed a good deal less likely if that platform had a crushed human being on top.

"How long do you reckon we've got?" asked the man.

Simon tried very hard to ignore the question. He couldn't help but notice that his watch still read 6.35am, meaning that only a minute had elapsed since the platform fell. In all likelihood, the dust hadn't even finished settling on the pavement, but there were still twenty or twenty-five minutes to go before the chances of being spotted began to improve even slightly.

"There's no avoiding the fact that we'd be a lot better off had this happened at, say, 8.00am," said the other man. "Rush hour is our greatest hope. What do you say, a thousand people working in this building, many more working nearby? I can't help thinking that it's inevitable that someone will spot us around eight."

"I suppose," said Simon, really regretting leaving his phone on the kitchen table.

"Which means that all we can really do is wait until then."

"What else could we do?" said Simon.

"We might fall," said the man.

Those were the exact options Simon had established himself, but there was now, he realised, a third option. Were one of them to fall before the other, then the chances of that other one being spotted increased, just as they would have done had one of them not managed to cling on to the crack in the glass and fallen with the platform. Simon decided not to mention this. He pinched still tighter with his fingers and congratulated himself on having maintained his athletic build into his late twenties. The other man was, from what Simon could see, older and perhaps therefore not as strong. It was hard to be sure, but it looked like he had a little goatee beard pressing up against the glass. That had to be irritating to some degree.

"Do you have a wife or girlfriend waiting down there?" asked the man.

"No!" said Simon. "If I had someone waiting down there, I'd like to think they'd be arranging our rescue right away."

"No, not down there on the ground," said the man. "I mean, down there in general? Out there in the city?"

Simon was unsure if he did or did not have a girlfriend right now. One of the other decisions he'd made that morning was to prefer not to know, to not consider the issue for a day. Right now it felt like he could really use one—a girlfriend that is—but it seemed best not to lie to the other man.

"No," he said, "not really."

"You know," said the man, "my wife says I snore too much. Every morning I wake up and get told, *Julius, you snored like an effing train last night, if you keep this up you'll have to start sleeping in the spare room.*"

Simon noticed that the time had finally ticked on to 6.36am. He worried that the increased strength of his grip that he squeezed when he realised that it was less a case of hanging on until he was spotted and more a case of hanging on longer than this man— who was apparently called Julius—was in fact a mistake. There was a delicate balance of pressure and strain running through his fingers that it was not in his interests to disturb. It was also highly annoying listening to Julius talk about his wife, but Simon hoped that the more he talked, the less Julius would be thinking about the balance of stress in his fingers.

"If I was to fall," Julius said, "don't you think that just a tiny bit of my wife might be glad? Every night, when she did get to sleep, she would sleep that little bit deeper."

"Yes, maybe," said Simon, deciding now to keep the man talking without really paying any attention to what he was saying.

Of course, as soon as Simon decided this, the man went strangely silent. It seemed that every decision Simon took on the 80th floor was a decision that this man was determined to mess up. Suddenly Simon was worried that the man had decided to stop talking and devote his undivided attention to the balance of pressure that held his own fingers to the crack in the glass. Simon, meanwhile, was thinking only about the silence and worrying that Julius' whole conversation about his wife was just a ploy to distract Simon from *his* fingers. Simon realised that his watch now read 6.38am. This meant that the man had been silent for twice as long as he had spoken. Desperately, Simon refocused on his grip. There were occasional gusts of wind that caused his arms to brace. Simon took the decision to keep his fingers tight but let his legs and torso sway slightly with the breeze. By swaying with it, not against it, energy and grip might be conserved. Julius was surely not going to think of that.

The silence, however, remained troubling. Simon began to wonder whether Julius might silently have fallen, whether he might in fact already be pressed against the pavement, his blood snaking into the gutter, pedestrians screaming and dropping their takeaway coffees before looking up at where the man had fallen from to see Simon still hanging on, delicately matching his body to the shape of the wind and the glass cold against his face.

Slowly, Simon turned his head to the right once more. It took perhaps thirty seconds to do it without disturbing his grip and each time a gust of wind picked up, he stopped and concentrated on swaying gently with it. When he finally got his head round, his watch read 6.38am and the man was still there.

"Hello again," he said.

"Hello," said Simon.

Simon's fingers were turning slightly blue.

"Have you ever wondered how birds are able to sleep on their perches without falling off?" the man asked.

"Yes, I have," said Simon. "Isn't it to do with their leg muscles?"

The other man ignored Simon and carried on.

"Their leg muscles are at rest when their claws are—"

"I know," Simon shouted. "I said I know this!"

Simon was now desperate for this man to be quiet. All he could think about was shutting this guy up.

"All I was trying to suggest," said the man, sounding hurt, "was that if we were birds we would probably find it easier to relax up here."

"If we were birds," screamed Simon, "we would just fly away!"

The man began to laugh. "Yes! Yes, we would." He shook his head to himself. "How dumb. Obviously we would just fly away."

The man continued to laugh, long after he had finished speaking. Simon found he was able to focus on his grip despite the laughter. He hoped that the laughter might dislodge the man and he wondered if he might be able to get him to laugh again. His watch now read 6.39am.

"Hey," said Simon. "I've just remembered a joke. Do you want to hear it?"

"Sure," said the man. "Fire away."

"There are these two guys out in the jungle who come across a tiger and one of the men starts frantically strapping on running shoes. 'What are you doing?' says his friend. 'You can't outrun a tiger.' 'I don't have to,' replies the first man. 'All I've got to do is outrun *you*.'"

There was total silence on the 80th floor. A small gust of wind caught Simon by surprise and he tensed. The fingers on his left hand squeezed hard and Simon felt them slide towards the lip of the crack only millimetres away from coming free entirely. He breathed in and out heavily. The joke did not appear to have gone down well. On reflection it was not necessarily the best joke to have told. Perhaps, given the context, it might not even have come across as much of a joke at all.

"What I don't get is why he would even have running shoes with him, if he was in the jungle?" said Julius.

Simon sighed. "Sorry," he said, "but why are you up here?"

"The same reason as you. The platform fell."

"But why were *you* on the platform?"

"I was looking for the window cleaner. I was sent to tell him to stop cleaning the windows because the wind was due to pick up and the management considered it too dangerous. We tried ringing him but couldn't get through, so I was sent up to find him."

Simon closed his eyes and let his face press against the cold glass.

"Why are you up here?" asked the other man.

"I was cleaning the windows."

It was 6.39am.

Purchase

KATIE AND I MET to talk about our purchases. We were each having problems, although I was having issues with trousers and she was having trouble with fish.

"REMEMBER WHEN IT WAS EASY TO BUY SALMON," she'd texted me earlier that week.

"What happened," I asked, adding an emoji of a fish leaping across the crest of a wave.

Katie replied with a crying heron and a post box, followed by: "EVERYTHING COMES WITH A FUCKING HERB CRUST."

I tried hard to console her. I made a meme of a sumptuous fish supper, using an old photo that was in black and white. Beneath the photo I wrote: "The good old days of fish." I think I thought that by placing fish suppers firmly in a shared past I'd make it clear that the problem with the herb crust was something we all faced. Katie replied with a rabbit that was doing a creepy wink. I was worried. Had my nostalgia come across as obtuse?

The next day I bought a new pair of trousers. They were not my usual style but the sales assistant convinced me.

"They'll look great with a plaid shirt," she said through chewing gum.

The label said they were based on an old design worn by foundry workers. Only as I was paying £110 for them did I realise that I had no idea what a foundry was.

Later, at home, I tried the trousers on and typed "foundry" into Google. I discovered that a foundry is a factory that produces metal castings and that the trousers themselves were made from a thick, brown canvas that was heavy and stiff. I messaged Katie a picture of the trousers and a link to the Wikipedia article about foundries. She replied with a film of a sweet factory where hot sugar was being rolled into a sausage.

"What are you up to?" I asked.

"Lunch."

"What are you having?"

"Crayfish salad—but I think the crayfish is off."

I sent her an emoji of a yellow face throwing up green sick.

KATIE'S PROBLEMS WITH FISH had been going on for some time, but the trousers only became an issue when I tried to wear them to work. They were okay to walk in, but as soon as you sat down the coarse material became tight across the calves and groin. Presumably if you worked in a foundry they were fine, but in the office they were uncomfortable.

The sales assistant was still chewing gum as I walked in. "No good?"

"They're fine," I lied, "but I think I need something lighter."

She helped me find a pair of trousers that were so light that when she passed them to me it felt like they were hardly there at all. Greek fisherman's trousers, the label said. I was in a rush so I paid the £79 and left.

Back at the office there was another email from Katie showing a mackerel fillet lying on a plate.

I replied: "tasty ;-)"

Katie sent an angry face followed by: "i didn't know it was smoked."

To cheer her up I explained about the foundry trousers being so stiff I'd had to buy something else.

"Now I get why you sent me that Wikipedia page," she said.

But the fisherman's trousers turned out to be enormous. According to the label they were modelled on ancient Greek fishing attire and were ideal for summer. Apparently fishermen would tuck the loose hems into their socks, but when I tucked them into my socks it made me look as if I was about to perform a rigorous national dance.

I sent Katie a picture with the caption "ANOTHER DISASTER" before going back to the foundry trousers and creaking my way to work.

That evening Katie put her laptop in the cupboard so we could Skype while she washed up. I made the mistake of asking after her dinner.

"I don't want to talk about it."

"That bad?"

"Crab sticks."

I began looking for a suitable meme to cheer her up, but then I realised we were on Skype so she would be able to see me browsing and not looking at the right window. In fact when I clicked back Katie was looking right at me.

"You should return those trousers," she said firmly. Then she declared she had to go to bed. "I'm due at Billingsgate at four."

BACK IN THE SHOP the next morning I decided on jeans. I found a table full of them and began to look for my size. There were many different styles, with abstract names like "Skinny Bill" and "Black Siren." I clutched at denim and realised I was close to tears. At some point the sales assistant took my arm.

"Can I help you?"

"What would you recommend someone who works for the council but likes to take walks over lunch?"

The sales assistant swallowed her gum.

When I got home I slept, dreaming that the new jeans were too tight and praying that they were the kind that stretched out as you wore them.

At around four Katie sent me a gif of a man walking through a door but always emerging in exactly the same room that he'd left. I asked about Billingsgate. She replied with ten sad faced emojis and an upside-down whale.

We met later outside a pub, me in my jeans and Katie clutching a large bin bag.

"How are your trousers?"

"Too tight."

We talked about our purchases as we walked down to the river carrying the bag full of fish. At the edge of the water we stopped and threw the fillets in one by one. I took off my trousers and hurled them into an open skip. We drank wine that we stole from the off licence and walked swiftly through the late evening rain, and we dreamt of a new economy, one based on gifts and not purchase—one where she chose my trousers and I bought her fish.

Stan, Standing

STAN, STANDING on the rug by the mirror by the door, nursing a weighty head cold that's come up sudden overnight, drinking coffee from an unwashed mug, staring at his reflection in a mirror that once belonged to his mother's brother, but which has been a mainstay in the hall by the door since Stan moved into the flat two years previous when his parents dropped round a job lot of his uncle's things—including the mirror that Stan's at now—all on account of Uncle Al having downsized, heavily, again, after another still more devastating divorce that no-one wanted to discuss yet, especially given how cut up Uncle Al had been over his first divorce, a stretch of time that involved weeping and mealtime silences and Stan getting home from school to find his mother and her brother sat out on the cold patio so that Uncle Al could smoke, something Stan's mother never let him do in her home even if Uncle Al clearly did so in his, or at least had done when he owned the mirror Stan's looking in on now, with that yellowing toward the edge and those stray burn marks on the frame as if Uncle Al did—as Stan suspects he did—stare himself down in the mirror as he smoked, before stubbing out on the frame and storming from the house, a thought which Stan finds concerning as he looks in on the mirror, sipping, sniffing, standing, wondering about today being the day of *his* brother's wedding.

Reaching out to place the unwashed mug on the cabinet that stands between the rug and that hallway mirror, Stan finds that his left arm is some five inches shorter than his right. Jesus, thinks

Stan, flexing those left-hand fingers and pushing the coffee cup a little further onto the cabinet. How can I only be noticing this now? Stan spends time looking down the lengths of each arm, his right palm resting on the cabinet, his left hanging loosely in mid-air. Perhaps this is why I've never got on with ties, Stan thinks, already wondering if he'll be able to bail out and go open collar. That said, with the news that his left arm is some five inches shorter than his right, on top of the way the head cold has him spinning and desperate to sneeze, Stan can't help but picture how disappointed his mother'll be when she finds out that while her oldest *has* arrived at his little brother's wedding he *has not* arrived with tie. "I thought it was open collar," Stan'll say, desperately trying to avoid bringing up how close he is to sneezing. "Given the time of year." Stan's mother'll frown, her new hat pinned tightly to her head, her left hand lifting slightly to gesture to all the other men in the room, all of whom will be wearing ties, none of whom will have colds, and *all* of whom, Stan reckons, will have arms of roughly, if not exactly, the same length.

The suit jacket that's hanging from the back of the door, and which Stan's standing in the hallway making ready to put on, has a rip in the lining. The suit also belonged to Uncle Al, dropped round by Stan's parents alongside the mirror. Stan fears his mother'll spot the dodgy lining and give him hell for rubbing it in Al's face. "Today's not easy for Al," she'll say, "The last thing he needs right now is to see what a mess you've made of his possessions." It must be disheartening for Al, thinks Stan. Nothing can actually be done about the ripped lining, just as nothing can be done about Uncle Al's regular divorces, constant downsizing, and general rough time of it. Standing on the rug, Stan decides that he'll try and flaunt the split lining a bit, to attempt to do as he thinks his Uncle Al deep down surely wishes, i.e. to not let his uncle's life be another elephant in another room, but rather to act as if having an elephant about is a real shit show and is ruining his uncle's life, along with the lining of Stan's suit.

Stan's been standing for perhaps thirty seconds, possibly even a minute. Without warning, the sneeze that's been at the back of his throat since he got to the mirror rises and threatens to emerge only to disappear, somewhere between Stan's tongue and teeth. Stan's mother'll be livid. She'll think that this sneezing and coughing is a deliberate ploy on the part of Stan to ruin his brother's big day. "When you have a wedding of your own you can cough as much as you like," she'll hiss as the organ voluntary picks up pace. "But until that day you can belt it and let your brother get married in peace." Stan knows that his mother is an irrational woman and that she'll be equally affronted if he was to turn up chewing on cough sweets. Her lower lip'll drop and she'll tap her husband, Stan's Dad, on the shoulder with the service sheet. "You know your son has only gone and brought sweets to his brother's wedding." Stan's affection for chewing is longstanding. As a ten-year-old he blew fifty pounds of Christmas money on a year's supply of gum. His mother declared the matter obscene and refused to tolerate it. Privately, Stan's father told him to have a good chew to and from school and any other time Mum was out. "Everyone needs a hobby," he told Stan. "Yours might as well be gum." Stan stretched out the gum until late October. Today in the pew his father'll listen to his mother's concerns and try and fight Stan's corner as best he can. "At least he's not coughing," he'll say. "You're not telling me you'd prefer him to be coughing?" "Why can't Stan just come to his brother's wedding and sit down?" Mum'll respond, leaving Dad lost for words, staring up at the priest as he looms over them from the chancel. Stan's Mum'll tut heavily and applaud at the end of the voluntary. On the far side of Stan's Dad, Uncle Al'll be leant over the pew, praying perhaps, or simply thinking about some other moment in his life.

Reaching for the jacket, Stan pulls it on and looks ahead into the mirror. There is nothing behind him worth speaking of. Even the wallpaper is plain, no puffs or creases or evidence of joints. Stan's been found out by wallpapering. In their early twenties he and his brother rented a place together. The Marchmont Road flat was in a bit of a state when they took it on so they decided to try and spruce it up. "I've spoken with the landlord," Stan's brother told him, "and he's okayed anything that's not structural." The brothers chose a wallpaper and Stan mixed up a paste. "I fucking love decorating," Stan's brother kept saying. Only when the wall was coated in paste, with the paper stuck in undulating folds across it, did Stan realise why most people prefer paint. Stan crouched on the floor, tugging at the half-pinned paper, while his brother clambered up on a borrowed stool. "Steady, Stan," he kept saying, "steady." It was then that Stan's brother asked Stan something that took him totally by surprise. "Stan," he said. "What do you think Abraham and Isaac talked about on the way home?" It took Stan a while to figure out what his brother was on about, Bible study being thin growing up. When he did finally clock it, he was still lost for a response. It was typical of Stan's brother, to think that Stan gave a shit about a conversation that may or may not have happened in a desert many years ago, when Stan was up to his elbows in wallpaper paste.

Desperately staving off the sneeze, Stan recalls the padded cycling shorts he got his brother for his twenty-fourth birthday, back when they were both regulars at the Lansdowne Cycling Club. The shorts were padded across the arse and crotch, as well as being a very deep blue that reminded Stan of blueberry ice cream. Barry, an older, jocular man at the club, publicly assured Stan's brother that they were great shorts, whilst nursing a huge grin. Yet Stan never did get out of his brother how great those shorts actually were.

Uncle Al's first wife was a large woman who needed assistance getting in and out of cars. As Stan understands it, she met Al at a spring dance Al went to when he was staying overnight in Nottingham with work. No-one seemed to believe Al when he said he danced the night away with Cathy up in Nottingham. "I know she's a big girl," Al said during the wedding preparations, "but once she's on her feet there's no stopping her." "You just keep telling yourself that," Stan's Mum said as she licked shut the invitation envelopes. Stan was only three years old at the time. There was a band at the wedding but Uncle Al and Cathy stayed put at the top table. "Cath's got herself a jammy knee," said Al to his sister's insistence that they both get up there and show them all something. During the course of the evening, Stan crawled under the table to try and establish if Cathy's knee really was covered in jam. Even now in the hallway, staring himself down in the mirror, Stan can recall the moment Uncle Al's first wife's left foot crunched into his nose and he found himself hauled out from under the table to be held aloft by his new aunt. "This boy's been looking up my fucking dress," she screamed at her husband, his family, her family and assembled guests. Stan still worries, as he does now, standing on his uncle's rug, arranging the collar of his uncle's suit, fighting not to sneeze on his uncle's mirror that his Uncle Al may one day trace back all of his troubles to the day his oldest nephew looked up his first wife's skirt.

Stan's mother is known in her circles as obtuse. She has, in her time, spent hours boiling, baking, fisting, and moulding her behaviour to ensure as much. Stan has, in his own time, found this irritating. Folding down the lapels of his jacket, Stan's major concern is that the longer he stands on the rug, staring at himself in the mirror and fussing over the flash of suit lining, the more likely it is that he'll be late. His mother's voice looms in the hallway. "Think of other people, Stan. Think of your poor brother up there like a plum, desperately scanning the congregation for your face." "Oh, it's my *poor* brother now is it?" Stan says. From what Stan has seen of his brother in the last couple of years, Stan being around was nearly as much of a deal for him as Stan being full stop. Recently, Stan's brother has reacted with confusion at Stan simply showing up. "I thought we were going cycling today," Stan once said, leaning his bike up against the wall of his brother's new house. Stan's brother looked confused, almost as if he wanted to ask "Who are you, again?" but somehow knew it would be rude. Stan almost wished his brother had blurted it out so he could explain. "I'm Stan, remember? We grew up in the same house, we lived together on the Marchmont Road, we used to go cycling together all the time, and you once asked me what Abraham and Isaac talked about on the way home but I never gave you an answer because I didn't think it was a serious question."

Finally inside the jacket, Stan considers the suit itself. He reckons it's most likely a legacy of Uncle Al's third marriage, which saw him live in a large country house in Leicestershire. "It was a marriage of convenience," Al later explained. "She needed a visa, I needed someplace to live." The good thing about being married to a Russian oligarch's divorcée, as Stan saw it, was that Al finally got himself some good tailoring. Throughout the five-year marriage, Stan and his family would make regular trips to the Leicestershire pile to spend time with Uncle Al while Uskrulya was away on business. Uska, as Al called her, was in fact rarely around. Stan reckons he saw her twice: once on a Friday after Stan's Dad drove them up straight from school, when a tall lady came bustling out of the house and disappeared in a Ferrari; once three years later when Stan tried smoking for the first time, sneaking out of the East Wing to light up a stolen Sobranie on the left lawn. Stan recalls coughing a great deal before seeing a downstairs light flick on to reveal Uska pacing up and down in a maroon jumpsuit and rimless sunglasses. Stan could just make out Uncle Al's head sat back on the sofa as Uska marched back and forth. Nothing happened for Uncle Al in there with Uska, but Stan smoked three cigarettes while waiting to see if anything would. Uncle Al would later describe those five years as the happiest of his life. "She never loved me," he would often say, "but she didn't stop me having a good time." The jacket, once on, is supremely light and made of a very fine wool, and the reflection staring back at Stan is of Stan in his uncle's suit in his uncle's mirror, standing on his uncle's rug.

Standing in front of the mirror, running a tie between his hands and worried about sneezing the whole time, Stan fears that his nostrils have taken to flaring in the exact same way as Uncle Al's do, whenever he delivers bad news. Nostril flaring is something of a family trait. Stan's mother does it, his father does it, Uncle Al spends practically his whole time doing it. Only Stan's brother does not seem to flinch before he speaks. Stan wonders if maybe today he might break his duck, whether the magnitude of the occasion might get to him and his nostrils might flicker. There'll be no saving Stan's own nostrils later. He'll file out of the church and make his way towards the happy couple, his brother'll stand loosely with easy-set shoulders, his wife—who Stan knows to be a personal trainer—firm on her feet, both of them turning to look at Stan as Stan's nostrils blow out, right before he begins to speak.

Weeks ago now, Stan's mother took him aside and told him that it was unusual for the brother of the groom to be made best man. "Who ever said it was usual?" Stan asked. "I'm just saying," Mum went on, "it would be a rarity and not something you should expect." As it happened Stan was not the best man as both he and his mother predicted. Yet that conversation got Stan thinking. Hiding in his jacket pocket, written in blue ink, are a few words that Stan found himself writing, not necessarily to stand up and deliver to the guests, but to have with him just in case.

Still waiting on the sneeze, Stan's now watching himself pull the note from his pocket with the long arm, unfolding it right there in front of the mirror. His nostrils flare something silly as he reads the first line.

I want to take a moment of your time to talk about love.

The reception'll be busy, Stan has no doubt.

Uncle Al's always been one for cars. Even when he's been down on his knees both financially and emotionally, he's always managed to hang on to a set of wheels. Stan's own father once called him a petrol head. Harsh, thinks Stan, when you think about it.

Soon the sneeze'll come and then I'll go, thinks Stan.

Still standing, still staring, Stan figures that he'll have to rise from his seat amidst the buzzing of the reception and bang a spoon against his glass. Beside him Uncle Al'll have his eyes on Stan from the off, his own arms folded and stately, like a manager who's two goals up in football. Stan's often thought that rather than his mother listing what his Uncle Al doesn't need, and rather than Al exploring marriage after marriage, maybe his uncle just needs a pal to chat to once in a while. As Stan understands it, Al's wives have never really provided conversation. The fifth, Tracy, certainly talked a lot, but primarily about herself and her three children, to whom Al played the role of father for a little over a year. Stan recalls once visiting Al, Trace, and the brood. The children were darkly obnoxious and bullied the father that their mother had found them something silly. They referred to Al as "Tesco-Dad," either because they somehow got wind of the summer Al worked the meat counter or simply because they saw the marriage as selected from a shelf. In the short time Stan was with them, all three children gave Al a cup of tea with salt in and the eldest hid Al's shoes in the dryer. "They're not all bad," said Al, as he walked Stan to the station in his socks. "Last month the middle one helped me mend the broken arm on my darts trophy." Stan couldn't help but worry that darts trophy help or not, walking around barefoot in November was not doing his uncle much good. Trench foot, for one, seemed likely. All in all, Tracy was a long year for Al and everyone agreed that he was as well shot of Tracy as he was of anyone. Thinking back on it, Stan's not even fully sure Tracey and Al were actually married in the legal sense, but that isn't the sort of conversation Stan and Al have ever had. Instead, it's a conversation Stan finds himself having with himself, albeit in Uncle Al's mirror.

The more Stan thinks about Abraham and Isaac, the more he's convinced that there was a lot of silence on that no doubt long and tedious walk home.

Stan can just picture the way his mother's face'll drop: the brother of the groom, making a speech, does Stan listen? Yes, thinks Stan, I listen all the time.

Stan's hopping from foot to foot before the mirror, aware that he is increasingly likely to be late, but stuck rising from his seat to tap on the glass with his spoon. Stan's nostrils'll flare some for sure, just as they will outside the church, standing alongside his brother and his brother's new wife; Stan's brother looking directly at him, confusion seeping across his face, while Stan himself looks on at Mary, who works as a personal trainer and who Stan first saw at the Lansdowne Cycling Club helping an elderly lady onto a chair after a fall in one of the aerobics classes the club's gym put on. Stan had smiled some at her tenderness and made his way to the showers, thinking of that kind girl's hand on that old lady's shoulder as he let warm water rush past his eyes. Now that hand'll be resting on the hand of Stan's brother, who'll be looking quizzically at Stan outside the church while Stan's speech burns a hole in Uncle Al's pocket.

"The real truth of it," Stan's saying out loud to the mirror, "is that things don't seem to pan out the way you think. Or, in all honesty, the way you want."

Stan's very aware of being in his own hall. The rug soft and thick beneath his feet, the mug edging ever closer to the lip of the cabinet, the mirror stained and smudged and reflecting Stan back at Stan.

No-one'll ever know today how angry Stan's brother is capable of being. A brother who Stan himself has had to restrain, a brother who has done malicious things to guinea pigs, a brother whose own mother was openly so-so on throughout his mid-teens, a brother who in that Marchmont Road flat once punched Stan on the nose.

Stan pictures Isaac screaming Abraham down in the desert, saying, *You fucking what?* Over and over and over.

One arm being longer than the other, still.

And, Stan's brother's nostrils once being the ones doing all the flaring.

The paper is crinkling in Stan's hands. There is a long history of repression in the family. On his mother's side it is nigh on rife. Still, standing in the hallway in Al's old suit, looking in Al's old mirror, worrying about his arms and his speech and living on the verge of sneezing, Stan wonders if Uncle Al might in fact be the exception. Stan recalls the penultimate evening of Al's seventh marriage when Al got picked up by the police from a twenty-four-hour Morrisons. Uncle Al's seventh wife, Maureen, was there, stood by the head of the canned goods aisle, watching her future ex-husband hurl tins of cooked carrots and Irish stew and kidney beans from aisle end to aisle end. The tins collected at Maureen's feet like flowers at a traffic accident. "Just sing out when we've got enough," screamed Al. "Just sing out!" Maureen cried silently until the police came and led Al away. Maureen was a curious one. On paper she was normal. Stan can remember his mother's joy when she first met her, regularly using the word "lovely" throughout the brunch. In the car on the way home, though, she stared out of the window with a pallid face. Stan figured he could read Mum that day: Maureen might be lovely, sure, but she was marrying Uncle Al here and she was going to be his seventh wife.

All went swimmingly for Al and Maureen for two years, until Al cracked that day in Morrisons. "She thinks there's going to be a nuclear holocaust," Al wept. "She lives in constant fear that our amenities will be cut off and we'll be reduced to the status of savages." "Well, we're all a bit concerned about that," Stan's Mum said. "But how did you end up in Morrisons, throwing all those tins?" Uncle Al said that people weren't listening to what he was saying, it wasn't just a bit of concern: "Back at home, she's got cupboard after cupboard of supplies. There's no fresh food in the house. Imagine living in a house full of food that can only be eaten in an emergency?" Stan's Mum later said that she didn't think Al was good for women. "As his sister it pains me to say it, but he drives all of us to think only of crises." Standing in front of the mirror, struggling to hang on to his left arm, his tie and his impromptu speech, Stan wonders whether Uncle Al is simply a man who throws tins when he's had enough of them rather than leaving them stacked up on the shelf.

"I want to take a moment of your time to talk about..."

In all likelihood there'll be near enough too much buzzing at the reception, Stan possibly struggling to be heard.

"A—A—CHOOOW!"

"...to talk about love."

Stan sneezes so violently he drops everything except his left arm. Sneezes are a strange one, Stan thinks, rising up suddenly with little in the way of warning, leaving no choice but to let the sneeze out. I've got a cold, Stan thinks. Why can't she deal with that? For a moment he is resolute. His mother'll have to lump it. She can take Stan as Stan is and if that involves a sneeze here or a speech there then she'll just have to accept that that is something Stan does, like chewing gum or cycling or not getting married.

With the jacket covering his wristwatch as it is, Stan's not in a position to be sure how much time has elapsed.

"I WANT TO TAKE A MOMENT OF YOUR TIME TO TALK ABOUT LOVE."

"You fucking what, *Dad?*" Isaac presumably said.

The fucking buzzing already.

Stan's mother claims to have spent most of her adult life waiting for her brother to die in a high-speed car accident. "I tell you, sometimes I just sit at home waiting for the call," Stan's mother told them all one Sunday last year when the whole family gathered at the behest of Stan's brother who wanted to announce some big news. "Come now Trudy," Stan's father had said, placing a hand near but not quite on Stan's Mum's shoulder. "Now's hardly the time." Stan's Mum shot Stan's Dad a look of fury. It was only in recent years that Stan had learnt that his father was a man who lived on thin ice, but if Uncle Al's marriages failed because he threw tins down the aisle at Morrisons, Stan's parent's marriage failed because Stan's Dad didn't. As it turned out Uncle Al didn't crash his car that day, although he did turn up with a screech of brakes and a garbled message about "fucking Diane"—Diane being Al's eighth and most recent ex-wife. Stan always figured that driving was something of a release for Al, a chance to commit his mind entirely to something that was not himself and his current marital strife. Stan imagines Al driving with very soft hands, focused solely on the road. Maybe if Mum went for the odd drive she too might soften slightly, Stan recalls thinking, right before his brother arrived with the big news. Later that same day Stan caught his Dad mending a saucer in the garage. "Don't tell your mother," he said, painstakingly piecing together some ten to twelve fragments of china. Stan could see that a section of the rim was missing altogether. Judging by the way his Dad's head hung over the Araldite it seemed like perhaps he knew too. "How did it break?" Stan asked. Dad didn't look up. "Your mother and I sometimes have what you might call disagreements," he said. "What do you call them?" asked Stan. "Your mother calls them debates," he said after a pause, "and I agree with her." The saucer was from a set that Stan's parents got given for their own wedding some thirty-two years earlier. Mum had been meticulous in maintaining it. "It's imitation Wedgwood," she would say, too often for Stan's liking. Mum was probably just jealous, Dad confided in Stan: "Al's got wedding china coming out of his arse."

"Love."

Diane was meant to be Uncle Al's Katherine Parr but she didn't make it.

"*You fucking what? Dad?*"

Stan taps the mug on the cabinet with the longer of his two arms so that the sound rings out in his hall.

Crease or no crease it looks like the tie'll be making an appearance of sorts.

Stan's brother has always been intrigued by awkwardness. That's why Stan's thinking that in many ways this'll be something of a treat. A present even. Stan still has the speech in his hands, his left holding the bottom, his right the top. Everything is silent. All buzzing has ceased. "Love," repeats Stan, hoping that his brother's nostrils'll be flaring. "That's what I want to talk about." Stan recalls the last full conversation he and his brother shared, walking back from what turned out to be the final time the two of them set off from the Lansdowne Cycling Club. "So Stan, have you got an answer for me yet?" Again it took Stan a moment to figure out exactly what his brother was on about. "Abraham and Isaac, what did they talk about on the way home?" Stan wanted to blurt out many things. His brother positively bounced beside him. "In all likelihood there was a great deal of silence," Stan finally said. "Really? You think there was silence? Because I think Isaac's going to have a lot on his mind." "Of course," agreed Stan, "but that doesn't mean it's all going to come billowing out on the walk home." At the entranceway to the clubhouse Stan's brother paused to glare at Stan. "His dad was seconds away from dashing his head in with a stone knife and he's only walking home because some voice called out from behind a bush. This isn't like when Mum started buying value crisps; you'd bring that shit up." Stan hopes there'll be some silence at the reception, plates of food half-eaten around them.

"You fucking what? Mum?"

Abraham and Isaac having recently eaten.

"What a lovely meal we're enjoying," says Stan.

Death Valley Junction

THERE WERE FIVE PEOPLE in the diner: a man at the bar with a motorbike helmet; a young couple over by the far window tittering at things on a camera; an old woman by the toilets with a small dog on her lap; and Jack sat back on the scuffed-leather bench, staring off into the desert. The server walked over slowly with a tray in his hands. This time the burger must be his. He didn't need to turn his head. He could taste it. The sweet bun, the soft patty, the salted cheese; lettuce, pickle, relish. Four times he'd seen that server emerge from the kitchen and four times his heart had leapt, his palms moistening at the thought that this time—surely—the tray would be placed in front of him. The first burger was for the biker who wolfed it down without ceremony. The second and third were for the couple who set upon their plates with urgency, ketchup and mayo staining their lips and a stray pickle landing on the strap of their camera. Jack was surprised to see the fourth taken to the old lady. She ate greedily, taking small rapid bites and picking out bits of beef from her teeth and slipping them down to the dog. Five people, four burgers. This one must be his. He stared out the window across the flat sand that shuddered in the midday heat. Breathed. Waited.

Before the burger reached him, Jack noticed movement out there in the desert. Something was approaching the roadside diner where everyone was eating a burger but Jack. At first he thought it was a car, but it was far too small. Then he wondered if it was a motorbike, but it wasn't moving nearly fast enough nor kicking up enough dust. As he waited for the server to lean past him and place the burger on the table, Jack realised that out there in the fifty-degree heat a man was running across the desert. Jack'd driven back that way only a few minutes earlier, screeching past the diner in a blur before realising he was desperately hungry. He hadn't passed anywhere for miles, nothing but flat dust and loose rubber from tyres that had burst in the heat, so he pulled the hire car to a halt, turned round and drove back. When he stepped from the SUV the sun grabbed hold of him and tried to throw him to the ground and by the time Jack staggered the twenty or so yards to the doors of the diner he was sweating and struggling to breathe. As he stepped into the diner the others briefly looked up at him but soon turned away. The server dragged himself over from the counter. Jack ordered the burger. Waited. Watching the runner Jack wondered how anyone could move in that heat, how anyone could even *think* of running, how they must have been running for many miles.

Jack was so focused on the runner that it took him a moment to realise that the fifth burger—his burger—had not yet reached his table. Instead the server was stood by the door, holding the tray in his hands and staring out of the window at the man running through the desert. Jack realised that the runner was now a lot closer. Would soon, in fact, reach the diner. His limbs were scarred by heat, but their motions were improbably smooth. Knees rose and fell, feet lifted and landed on the tarmac, no hint of the weight of the heat. The server was still stood by the door, the tray with the burger still in his hands, his eyes still fixed on the running man. Five people, five burgers, one runner. There's no way, Jack thought, that that burger can be for him? But there was the runner, nearing the diner, and there by the door was the server holding the tray.

"Hey," Jack called out. "That's for me, right?"

Everyone in the diner looked up except the server. The runner reached Jack's car, parked at the end of the lot. He was a lot older than Jack had expected. A wizened, gnarled figure. He strode through the heat of the desert and *still* the server stood by the door, holding the tray, waiting. Everyone else had long since finished. The biker was reading a newspaper. The couple were packing up their camera. The old woman dropped the last of her beef onto the tongue of her dog. Jack watched the runner as he reached the diner. He waited for him to make his way up the steps, to come in and claim the burger, but the runner didn't stop. Instead those limbs carried on gliding through the desert and when the server eventually moved it was not to bring the burger over to Jack's table, but rather to return the tray to the kitchen as if the whole thing had been a mistake.

A Sense of Agency

THAT THE WATER WAS RISING only became unavoidable when the puddle James stepped in turned out to be the Thames. He looked to me with the waterline at his knees, to ask me why I'd stopped. Ahead of us small waves rolled softly across the path. In truth I had known about the flood for several days, but eager not to ruin our walk I kept my mouth shut. While most of London was moving furniture upstairs and people with ground floor flats were ringing round relations with first floor rooms to beg for a stay that experts warned might be a matter of months, James and I met in Putney and picked our way past the queues of traffic fleeing the city until we found the path that ran alongside the river. People stared at us from their cars, as if we were insane, but if James noticed the sideways glances he didn't mention it. He referred to the wind as "bracing" and took the piss out of me for wearing a coat. The path was wet with glossy mud and leaf mulch. We walked in single file. I could hear James' rucksack rattling ahead of me and water nipping at the bank. Regularly, James would stop to look at his watch, turn his head towards the dense cloud and declare us not far off high tide.

We stopped for coffee at Barnes Bridge, finding a Nero whose employees were frantically ringing head office to ask if they really did have to stay. "Why are you here?" the girl asked us, her colleague still on the phone.

"For a cappuccino and a flat white," said James.

"You're mental," said the girl, as she dashed to make our drinks. She stared at us while we drank them until eventually she came over. "I'm going to ask you again," she said. "Why are you here?"

James became annoyed. "Listen," he said shortly. "I don't know what you want me to say, but where I'm from there's nothing weird about two pals popping out for a walk."

As he spoke the girl reached forward to place her hand on the tabletop, as if steadying herself against wind on a cliff. "Are your drinks okay?" she asked. Outside, thin rain was beginning to fall.

As it happened, the girl and her colleague got the okay to scarper around the time we left. I looked back to watch them lock the door and leg it in the direction of Wimbledon. James was already marching back towards the river, kicking through the puddles that lived at the side of the street. I let go of the queues of cars and the stares of the girl in Nero. Sure the Isle of Dogs might be three weeks under water, yes the O2 and the Greenwich peninsula were lost last weekend, with Canary Wharf, Rotherhithe and the City saved by defences rushed in by the army, but this was the path from Putney to Richmond, miles from the Thames barrier, with James smiling as we walked on in single file. We continued, until I was standing on the last bit of dry path I could see, watching him splash on towards Kew.

"It's residual dampness," said James, stomping about in the wash, "left over from spring."

James has often been what you might call stubborn. Once on holiday he refused to bring his passport, saying that he was entitled to travel on his driver's licence when entering and leaving the EU. It caused no end of problems but, after four hours at the French border and several bilingual phone calls, James was let through. Vindicated by bureaucracy. Five days later we did the whole thing again so he could get home. Mostly he'd prove himself right in the end, the passport being one instance, the time he refused to back down in a dispute over where his neighbour should park being another. But recently he'd been less fortunate. A few weeks ago I saw him through the rain eating takeaway food from a polystyrene box and demanding that he knew a man who cowered at the bus stop. I splashed my way through puddles towards him.

"I know you," he kept saying. "Don't call me a liar when I know you."

It was very late and if it wasn't for the rain I imagined the man would long since have left the bus shelter. As it was he was stuck there repeating that he was sorry but he really didn't think he'd ever met James before. "Bullshit," James said. "Total bullshit." He was wet through and the remains of his kebab floated in the inch of water that had collected in its box.

"James," I said. "What's going on?"

Rather than persist he simply changed the subject. "Sam," he slurred. "Aren't you excited for our walk?"

I said that I was and made small talk about the Thames path until the man managed to leap over the puddle and onto a 436.

"You know," James said, turning back again to find me still standing on the one bit of dry path I could see, "it's really not that far to Kew. Once we're in Kew, Richmond is only round the corner. Maybe we can stop for a drink?"

I noticed that the water was now above James' knees. The Thames washed ripples of loose waves across his thighs and through the gloomy sky I could make out a sailing boat that had come unmoored and was floating aimlessly on the river, rising and falling in the wind like a drunken swan. James stared at me as if I was mad. I knew I was expected to follow, to go on towards Kew and eventually Richmond, but that would involve stepping into water rising before my eyes. A wave splashed past the tree to James's right, nearly causing him to lose his footing and plunge in. Behind me water swallowed a small bush.

"Not a session or anything, just a couple of beers down by the riverside."

Melanie was an unnerving girl. Her eyes were ferocious and could cut through a room like a rudder. If you looked straight at her they could bear down on you and soon make you uncomfortable. She spoke surprisingly quietly, unless she was angry about something in which case she would shriek and bang tables with small, tight fists. I remember when we first met her, before she and James were going out, hearing those fists thump the table next to us, and turning to see this wide-eyed girl whispering excitedly to her friends. She dressed in agricultural shades of brown and green, with the occasional stone-grey scarf that hung like a ruined escarpment on a damp castle wall. Many piercings were inserted across her eyes and brow and she had a tattoo of Roger Rabbit eating a carrot that she described to me as "a rush of sixteen-year-old excitement." Melanie was political. She occupied, she sat in, she protested, she marched. I never knew what she did for a job, but there were rumours of a rich parent she hated. She never struggled for money. Last summer, just after James went freelance, she was able to pay most of his rent. She loved animals and would coo over unsuitable dogs. She'd bring up the plight of whales at times that I found annoying and if I spent too much time with her I began to yearn for a conversation that didn't end with Melanie thudding those fists onto the table seeking me out with those eyes and telling me that poaching or deforestation or people stealing eggs made her physically sick.

A lot of the people who I suppose would now strictly be called James' former friends mark the beginning of his troubles by the day Melanie turned to him and said they couldn't be together anymore because there was a rainforest in Nicaragua whose spider monkeys she simply had to defend. They said that James was suffering from a very normal bout of heartbreak, that Melanie was way out of his league, and that when she let him go he couldn't take it. But James has always been stubborn and it would be un-wise to lay blame at the door of someone as unnerving as Melanie. Besides, that was over a year ago; only recently did James become so elusive. He would fall silent for weeks at a time before show-ing up at my door unannounced, demanding that we visit the pub. Most of his friends grew tired of lending him money he never repaid or making arrangements he never kept, but I was always happy to find him on my doorstep with rainwater streaking through his hair and his glasses blurred with mist.

"Sam!" shouted James, his arms outstretched and parallel to the water. "It's not even raining that hard."

Late last summer, at the wedding of a mutual friend, I saw James climb onto a chair and shout across the reception. This was in the same month that the sudden housing slump shattered the dreams of many Londoners, but James was convinced that the recession was actually the work of property companies attempt-ing to reset the playing field for London housing in much the same way as it is possible to clear an etch-a-sketch by shaking it.

"Everyone seems so desperate to believe that this is simply happening," James shouted, a glass of Prosecco in hand, "but things don't just happen and this slump is the work of the very people who need you to believe this is fate we are dealing with!"

It was a strange move on James' part and a distasteful time to bring it up, the bride and groom having already lost the home they were due to move into. I watched my friend try to convert the room until a man called Steve caught the lower side of his jaw with a punch that saw him not only unable to speak but also struggl-ing to see.

"Don't you ever stop to ask yourselves why here? Why only London?" Then he ran off into the rain, clutching his bleeding chin with his hands.

"Sam!"

Then came the flood. There was talk of people buying tickets to gigs at Alexandra Palace and refusing to leave. People had taken to visiting Crystal Palace for days at a time. According to the news, Hampstead Heath had become a refugee camp overnight. James said it was hype. "People will believe anything," he said. "This is all about housing."

I asked him what he meant. Apparently, the whole thing was still the work of property developers, clearing whole swathes of the city by opening up the Thames barrier.

"Don't you think it's strange how much we're encouraged to freak out," he said, "but how little anyone is doing to stop it?"

James' few remaining friends said he was bitter because of losing his house but James lost his house long before the crash, when he went freelance and stopped turning up to work. I struggled to know where to stand, but I figured James needed a friend so I shelved my concerns and pretended that the drains could cope and that if we sat tight everything would soon return to normal. Every time I saw James in recent weeks he grinned and told me how excited he was about our walk. At some point after he went freelance, James gave up buying shoes.

"Sam!" James shouted, the water now at chest height. "Is this a walk or what?"

Eight years earlier, in the summer we both turned twenty-two, James and I walked the length of the Thames from the barrier all the way to Teddington. The sun shone sharply and no rain fell. Over one weekend we walked all day and drank all night, sleeping on friends' sofas and once in a park looking up at the stars.

"Don't you want to just keep walking?" James said. "On and on, to the source?"

Many times over the following years we promised ourselves we would do it again, but we never did. Sometimes I would go and walk a section by myself, most often between Putney and Richmond, where the river slims down to something across which someone with ambition might believe they could skim a stone. At some point we gave up trying to fit it in. Maybe we were just too busy or maybe we simply had better things to do. That was until a few weeks ago when James turned up on my doorstep with his shirt wide open, in shoes held together with Duck tape, saying hadn't we better go for a walk along the Thames before the summer was out? Summer wasn't really something to recognise— there had been perhaps two dry days since March—but James leant on my doorjamb and talked about the year we walked to Teddington and didn't I want to be getting out in the open air soon? Later in the pub we inked in a date and James made me drink until the early hours, ruining the next day at work. I asked him how freelancing was going and he said it was all bullshit and he didn't even understand advertising anymore. A company was suing him for breach of contract and he had no intention to fight it. At three am we crawled home through the rain, fighting our way across puddles. At some point the Duck tape on James' shoes peeled off and washed down a drain. As we said goodbye, with our clothes soaked through, I thought I'd better ask James if he was okay. He smiled. "I'm fine," he said. "I'm so gloriously fine." And I believed him. We hugged each other in the rain and I smelled the yeast on his breath and felt his beard against my cheek.

For four weeks I wondered if I would ever see James again, whether the arrangements we had made were simply part of another chapter in his chaotic life, whether come the morning he would even remember who I was and how he knew my name. I watched my friends either leave the city or rearrange their houses so that they could live upstairs. Everyone I knew had a rubber dinghy and a cupboard that was only tins. When I woke this morning to the news that the London Eye was not expected to last the day I considered stealing my neighbour's car and seeing if I could make it to my parents', but before I tried James sent me a message: "Putney, 9am :)"

I suppose you could call it denial. I suppose with James a foot away from being submerged and the four yards of dry ground I was standing on rapidly shrinking from sight you could say we *were* insane. I suppose the whole thing should be properly considered for the fuckup it surely was. Overhead thunder clapped the skyline and rain began to fall in thick drops that hit the water like shells.

Bill Mathers

THE NOVELIST, CRITIC, AND ANGLER Bill Mathers got on with the literary establishment only marginally better than he did with his own family. Throughout his career he resisted interviews, describing them as "mere archaeology." He lived out the final years of his life in a Richmond nursing home where he was placed—against his will—by his estranged son. While there he placed an advertisement in the local paper: *Old man, blinding writer. Seeks reader for short walks and zero conversation.* For two years I was lucky enough to be that reader. We would go out twice a week, first pushing his wheelchair around Kew Gardens on Tuesday afternoons, then along the Thames on Friday mornings. Both journeys would end in the White Grape where we would each drink a pint of mild. I would carry a copy of Malcolm Lowry's *Under the Volcano*, from which I would read as we walked, and a loaf of unsliced bread with which I would feed ducks. Initially, Mr. Mathers was near silent, only grunting at passages of Lowry or laughing at small waterfowl struggling with bread. Slowly, however, perhaps mindful of his ebbing mortality, he began to share a few thoughts. I collected his opinions in a small notebook, which after his death sat limp upon my desk for several months. I'm now sharing selections with you.

BILL MATHERS, 1934-2011

On Anthony Trollope: "Makes time spent reading Dickens look like an investment."

On William Shakespeare: "Old, but that's not the worst of it. He makes it look like old people can't spell."

On *Catcher in the Rye*: "People go through their whole lives thinking that's how you write a book."

On his mother: "An atrocious human being."

On Toni Morrison: "She looked at me once and made me feel very small. I probably should have left it at that."

On *Don Quixote*: "Apparently one summer the whole Real Madrid squad was made to read it, even Beckham, although I think they gave it to him in translation, a staggering achievement in itself."

On carp: "Never saw the point. I got fed one once in Italy; it tasted like shitty bream."

On Zadie Smith: "She farted once at the Booker ceremony, cleared the whole room. Still didn't win though."

On Ian McEwan: "You know he can't even drive? You shouldn't be allowed to write if you can't drive."

On Walter Benjamin: "People go around quoting him like he's a pal. They miss the point: you're not meant to think he's your pal."

On his Aunt Maureen: "She got arrested in '62 for GBH, the same day her husband got arrested for ABH. I remember my Mum laughing and telling me they were having a competition, but all I saw was a family who cared."

On Hunter S. Thompson: "Drank him under the table. He wouldn't admit it because he was a pussy and a lightweight, but he was chucking up on the hard shoulder while I was in the boot pulling out another Grolsch."

On pollack: "A lot of people will try and tell you it's as good as cod, but a lot of people will tell you that Howard Jacobson deserved the Booker."

On *Moby-Dick*: "I read it at school then forgot everything. Thirty years later I overheard a man talking about it in the waiting room at my local surgery. For half an hour I thought he was complaining about a new kind of venereal disease."

On Virginia Woolf: "*Mrs. Dalloway*, 7. *To the Lighthouse*, 4. *Orlando*, 2. *The Waves*, 5. The others I couldn't find."

On Ted Hughes: "Shit at fishing."

On his father: "He sold my school football shirt. I brought it home on Friday to wash and by Monday he'd sold it. I only cared because it wasn't so easy getting into teams back then."

On Jonathan Safran Foer: "I thought he worked in TV?"

On bass: "Like reeling in yards of glorious silk."

On Doris Lessing: "We shared a pizza once. I was about to offer her the last slice when she just grabbed it. I went straight home and burned her novels."

On his brother, Charles Mathers, a civil servant: "Thin, but not in a brittle, scrawny way. No. He was strong, what people called wiry before the internet. Also not a lot of people knew how bad *he* was with money."

On Marcel Proust: "Too short."

On Michel Foucault: "I met him once in Paris. He won't remember because he was so drunk and I can't really remember what happened after he hit me."

On pike: "I've broken three landing nets bringing in those angle-fuck-fish."

On Kingsley Amis: "Should have had the snip."

On George Orwell: "I saw all of his books once in a butchers, every one of them, alphabetised on a shelf, above the bacon and ham."

On his grandparents: "They thought my father was soft for not sending me to boarding school so they'd re-create the experience when I stayed in the summer. Fed on bread and water, hours of Latin verbs, and then bed in dorms full of local children my Grand-dad paid to tease me. I ran away in my second term."

On Ernest Hemingway: "A whole generation thought it was cool to drink while you fish because of that clown."

On Rainer Maria Rilke: "It got very fashionable didn't it. Liking Rilke. Everyone would titter in the corner at parties and say things like, 'Rilke, now *there's* a poet.'"

On Dodi Smith: "I watched her once hit a policeman. I was there, interviewing him for the *Daily Express*. She came from nowhere. Huge amounts of blood. It was settled out of court."

On Julian Barnes: "All I'll say is that there's this guy in the IRA who's in love with him, as in madly in love with him, but Julian's too much of a fucking prude."

On E.M. Forster: "If you go to his grave you can see it rotate 365 degrees every time they announce the Booker shortlist."

On bream: "Too slippery by half, but lush if you can land them."

On his mother: "She gave me a London Underground map for my fourteenth birthday. She'd highlighted all the stops where you could sleep rough. I'd just started thinking about becoming a writer, not properly, but you know buying pens and so on. She thought she was being exceptionally funny but that map came in real handy."

On Lydia Davis: "I was in love with her for ages, then I read her stories and realised that that was the point."

On prawns: "If you show me how to catch a prawn I'll burn my rod."

Above the Fat

His hand hovers above the hot fat—not so hot as to be spitting and scarring his skin, but warm; warm enough to cook something; warm enough to be tender; warm enough for an egg.

The egg is inside his hand. He checks the temperature of the gas and makes a minute adjustment. If the fat is too hot when the egg hits the pan it will burn; the white will turn to rubber, the yolk will split. No. The fat must not be so hot as to do damage. He adjusts the temperature once more, the blue ring of gas shrinking ever so slightly, his hand motionless above the fat, the egg inside its shell, the fat itself thick and motionless, waiting.

Behind him in the sink is another pan, hurled in anger moments earlier after he came back to the kitchen from the freezer to find the first egg ruined. In an hour or so a boy of fifteen or sixteen will show up and find the pan upside-down in the steel basin where the burnt egg may have slid towards the plug, the oil no doubt splattered across the clean walls of the sink. He has no idea how it landed. He didn't look. He just hurled it across the room in anger, letting the industrial clang of metal on metal ring out through the silent kitchen. He swore, probably, but he can't be sure what he said. All he knows is that before the ringing had even stopped he took another pan from the shelf above the hob, placed it on the ring, filled it generously with fat and took an egg from the tray, holding it—as he still does—above the fat, waiting for the temperature to be *just* right, waiting so that he can be sure to have control over the cooking and won't be playing catch-up with a hot pan, determined to get this right.

Soon the boy—whose name he forgets—will turn up and be angry. He'll see the sink with the burnt pan and moan. He'll moan about the mound of washing up stacked beside him, he'll moan about the potatoes he must peel, the spinach he must wash, the cheese he must cut and move out of the fridge to the shelf where it can come to room temperature. In the past the boy has forgotten to move the cheese and this has led to confrontations. The boy has been talked down to about responsibilities and the precarious nature of his employment—"Shouldn't you still be in school?" the landlord said. "Shouldn't you be bothering someone else's workplace?"—but the landlord's condescension won't stop the moaning. The boy will walk through the back door any minute now in his white trainers and spotless peaked cap and moan. In truth there are two boys and he is never sure which one will turn up. It is something of a lottery with the boys. Sometimes they show up at ten, exactly when he asked them to arrive, but at other times eleven, sometimes twelve; occasionally they both show up at once and he has to send one of them home; and a few times neither of them has shown up at all, both later claiming to have had no idea they were meant to be working. The landlord spat blood. They would be fired, he said. They were insolent. They were good for nothing. They were beyond all kinds of pale. They should be in fucking school. In the kitchen, though, he is more sympathetic. It is not impossible that they are right and he is wrong, that he did not in fact tell them when they were working, or that maybe he told the wrong boy or forgot to tell them entirely. There are two boys, remember, so it can be confusing. Besides, from what he can tell, both boys—whatever their names—spend a lot of their time stoned. During their afternoon breaks they invariably disappear up the lane to the field, returning half an hour later, clothed in a sweet, organic aroma, their hands focused intently on the warm water in the sink. For this, too, he is sympathetic. He knows that if you are sixteen there isn't all that much to do out here other than get stoned. If he knew about the boys taking their breaks up in the field, the landlord would no doubt call the boys idiots, good-for-nothings, wasters, just as his own father in turn once called him an idiot, a good-for-nothing, a waster, when he himself, aged sixteen, spent much of his time stoned. So: no. The boys getting stoned is not something to worry about. It is to be expected and it should also be expected that stoned people are sometimes late or forget that they are meant to be working or don't show up.

HE FIGURES he must have been around the boys' age when his own father began to dislike him. Dad was a respectable man. A solicitor. A parish councillor. A reader of local planning applications. An organiser of fêtes and in weekly attendance at church. Around the age of fifteen or sixteen, though, his father began to look at him as if he were a weed peering through the soil of his garden; a stain on his white tablecloth; a speck of mould around the Belfast sink.

"Why does Dad hate me?" he asked his mother—an upstanding woman in her own right, although too often, he thought, lying down; stuck in her room, on her back, surrounded by pillows and well-wishers' cards.

"He doesn't hate you," she would reply. "He loves you very much."

But she was unwell and so she didn't know how things moved in the kitchen. The old man's eyes traced a line around his teenage frame and tried to cut him from the room. It seemed easiest to oblige him. He would stay out late with a friend whose mother worked nights. They smoked a bit of pot. It was something to do.

"You're a criminal," the old man had told him. "I'm a solicitor, in case you forget. I can't believe you'd bring drugs into my home."

"It's just a bit of pot, Dad."

He was grounded. No doubt fined pocket money he did not yet have. Angry at the injustice, he fought back. He remembers breaking free from his bedroom window, walking five miles to a party and falling asleep in a vacant playing field. When he returned his old man listed the moments in which he had been stupid, the points when he might well have died. Sanctions swirled around the house as the old man tended to his herbaceous borders.

Of course now, looking back, he can see that he did nothing to help matters. He would go out of his way to wind the old man up. He remembers once mowing the lawn and running the blades of the mower straight over the flowerbeds, shredding the old man's marigolds until everything was mulch.

"You're an animal," the old man said when he found him. "Sometimes I'm not sure I know who you are."

"Fuck you," he said.

As soon as he could drive he saved up for a car and as soon as he had a car he left.

HE MOVES HIS HEAD SLIGHTLY, lowering his knuckles towards the fat as if plumbing for depth. He adjusts the gas. The egg in his hand is warming slightly just as the eggs in the tray are warming slightly on the counter where he placed them after he removed them from the walk-in fridge. Really he should not be wasting his time frying eggs, but instead breaking twenty of them into a bowl to make a custard tart. He has the pastry—made the day before—already on the counter. The cream and milk and sugar are right where he left them before he went to the freezer to pull out the five bags of peas he'd decided, suddenly, to turn into pea soup. Nothing special, simple pea soup, served with sour cream and watercress in a tiny bowl or maybe even a coffee cup. Not even something to put on the menu, just a way of clearing space in the freezer as well as letting the people who ate in the pub that evening know that everything was going to be okay. Or at least that was the idea that

struck him just after he cracked the first, ill-fated egg, when he
remembered all those peas taking up space in the freezer and
thought how well they would go with the fresh watercress he
would send the boy to collect from the river—because it was all
well and good to moan about how not one of his customers would
know good food if it bit them, but what he should really be doing
is educating them, and that was what the pea soup would do with
its gentle sweetness and sour cream and bitter crunch of watercress—it would educate them—because people are scared of
things they don't know and stick to patterns that are predictable
and limited and safe. To educate, you have to change those patterns. That's what the pea soup would do. It would say, don't worry,
the food you are about to receive is for *eating*; it is not an idea, it
is not a promise, it is nourishment—and nourishment is what
tastes good, not buckets of trash or white plates of pretension—
and pea soup hit him as just about the archetype of nourishment;
it was not *cordon bleu*, it was not from a can, it bridged the gap; it
was *pottage*, full and whole and wholesome, people's food, eaten
by peasants in medieval fiefdoms, and *that*, he decided on the
way back from the freezer, his hands numb from carrying five
bags of peas, *that* is exactly what he will call it—*pottage*—and no-
one will pay for it, it will sit on the hob and be sent out ahead of
the starters to educate people, to set the tone, to let them know
that everything is going to be okay, and he smiled to himself as he
carried those peas and laid them on the counter and he remembered the mint that grew in the garden two doors down that he
would appropriate next time he nipped out for a fag, and he hoped
that if whichever boy turned up today was feeling sharp maybe
he could take charge of the *pottage* during service and that would
be his job for the night and he might, in turn, find some worth in
doing it, and maybe see a future beyond turning up late and piss-
ing off the landlord; and he reached for the big pan almost with
glee, diving under the counter for bay leaves and onions and

leeks, and only when he saw the burnt egg did his smile drop as he hurled the pan across the room, the overdone egg hammering into the sink because who ever changed anything with pea soup?

GOOD FOOD was the one bridge that crossed the ferment between them. For ten years he and his father had only met over lunch, a series of long meals at which the two of them sat in silence perusing menus as they yearned for the waiter to bring a semblance of relief.

"Steak rare," the old man would bark. "With béarnaise."

The waiter would turn to him. "The same."

Some fathers would smile. Not his. They returned to the culture of fury that weaved a seam across the tablecloth.

"What are you doing for money?" Dad would inevitably ask.

He would shrug. "This and that."

The steaks would arrive, the old man paring meat and lifting it to his lips. He bit. He chewed. He swallowed.

"You'll need more than this or that to keep you in steaks and béarnaise."

He wonders now if the old man's barbs were responsible for him enrolling at technical college at the age of twenty-six and deciding to train as a chef. Either way, Dad was resolutely indifferent. He'd trained in London but he didn't stick around because everyone said that to be taken seriously you needed to have worked in France. He arrived in Paris knowing very little and left knowing a lot. He moved to Spain. Back to London. To New York. Collecting references and menus. There was a girl in Paris. Another one in Madrid. One in New York who actually meant something. They talked of taking their knowledge to a smaller town and having a life together. It didn't work out. Last he heard she was making preserves and selling them in Williamsburg markets. Their email exchanges were terse. Options were slim. He came back to England and drifted in and out of work. With his experience he found he could walk into certain jobs, but just as easily walk out. A friend from Madrid said she was making a killing knocking out five-course meals in Chelsea dining rooms as a private chef. He agreed to help. The guests were excruciatingly vacant and their host thought it was hilarious to give them their tips in cocaine. He did not go back. He was done with the city where food seemed to be nothing but small plates of ideas. It was theatre. It was perfume. No-one got fed. No. London was done. Spain was too bankrupt. He worried he'd forgotten most of his French. The emails from Williamsburg were few and far between. There were other places to explore, sure, but in truth he was done with new.

He returned home. The old man was older still with grey hair that thinned to a scalp and hands that held fast to furniture. They ate lunch in the village pub, breaking the silence to agree that the food was a disgrace, before retreating to their respective sides of the table as lines of locals munched on burgers and buckets of chips. They must have said about ten words apiece while they were eating, one for each year he'd been away.

"Food used to be all right here," the old man said, getting up from the table, hands pressed on the back of his chair. "But it's gone downhill."

He shuffled off. As they left, the landlord explained that the chef had quit and run away to Malta.

"Malta?" the old man said.

For two nights he lay in his childhood room and resisted. Then he gave in. He pulled together a CV. He almost crossed out a few places. He assumed no-one round here would have heard of Per Se. He was wrong. He was given a kitchen and two fifteen-year-olds who would alternate doing dishes. The rest was up to him.

"How many covers do you usually do on a Saturday?" he asked.

"Depends." The landlord shrugged.

"Depends on what?"

"On who comes in."

HIS KNUCKLES ARE WARM NOW, not hot, but warm, so with care he lifts his hand and taps the egg on the side of the pan—disturbing the fat ever so slightly—and carefully with two hands he opens the egg along the crack, barely a centimetre above the fat and lets the transparent gel spill out onto the surface where it does not bleach, but lies still, in the fat, and he lowers his hands still further with his knuckles all but in the oil so that the yolk, when it comes, does not fall and break, but rather slides softly into the small island he's built in the fat, and as soon as the egg is out of the shell his hand whips away and the shell flies across the room in the direction of the bin, but his eyes never stray from the egg in the pan, watching intently, already thinking about adjusting the heat, worried that it is too hot, but not yet, he must wait, he must give the egg time to settle because if he makes big changes too soon he'll have another burnt egg on his hands and once burnt there is nothing that can be done for them.

THE OLD MAN did not come on the opening night. Nor the next night. Nor even the following week. When he did show up it was lunchtime on a Tuesday. The boy who was meant to be washing up that day had failed to show and so the first meal he ever cooked for his Dad was served amidst chaos and recrimination. He only realised the old man had been in when he went out for a cigarette and saw him shuffling across the carpark. For a moment he could hardly believe it was him, then he couldn't believe he hadn't so much as poked his head round the kitchen door to pass judgment. When he asked the waitress about the old man's demeanour, she said he'd just eaten the meal and left.

"Fuck him," he said.

He scratched around. He took a flat in town where it was cheaper and there were more pubs where he could drink. He looked up some old friends. He found them older and more tired than he expected. Some were married. Others divorced. Nearly all of them had kids, except one who was killed in a car accident. It was the same friend whose mum worked nights, with whom he would go and get stoned. Apparently he'd been driving home late from the pub and wrapped his car around a tree. One evening after service he found tears in his eyes as he tidied the kitchen. The next morning he found himself watching the boy—forgiven for now—peeling potatoes in the deep sink, wondering if *he* had friends who one day might disappear. He strained his memory for details. He recalled smoking joints in a tree house and riding bikes downhill. He found a photo online, alongside an article about the crash, but he could not recognise the face he saw and he had no idea at what point they last spoke.

He drifted on, his memories tugged by the pull of the present. He found someone to sleep with. She was younger. So much younger that he didn't dare ask in case the answer brought up the question of how old he now was. Hers was another world. They had no mutual friends. When she found out he was a chef she demanded he cook her something. He fried her an egg. A week later she disappeared to Thailand. "I go every winter," she said.

THE FIRST THING HE LEARNT when he arrived in Paris was how to fry an egg. There was one way to do it, the head chef explained; he would show him only once and after that every egg that was cooked in his kitchen would be fried in exactly the same way to the exact same standard, otherwise it would be thrown out. "A hen can only lay one egg a day," the chef told him, "so an egg is a whole day's work for the hen. You burn one egg, you're on a warning. You burn two and you're gone." He can still hear that old French chef's instructions now as he watches the pan. He knows that frying an egg to perfection is all about controlling the heat. At times it will cook too fast, at others too slow, but if he is reactive he can manage these imperfections. He has to keep the egg off the ground almost, floating above the fat, letting it rise and fall, moving the pan back and forth across the heat, adjusting the gas to keep the egg safe, the transparent gel faintly bleaching now against the black non-stick pan and the yolk starting to hold itself tighter.

HE KNEW SOMETHING HAD CHANGED the day he went home to pick up some clothes and found the old man with a can of soup. It was late autumn and Dad had the tin open in his lap in the living room, drinking the soup in short sips as he stared at the blank television screen. It was impossible to tell if he'd recently turned the TV off or was about to turn it on when he was interrupted, but the soup was the biggest shock. It was cream of tomato. He stared at the tin for a long time before he spoke.

"What are you doing, Dad?"

The old man smiled. "Hello," he said. "Do you want to try some of this soup?"

A red droplet was caught on the millimetre of grey bristle that was attached to his top lip. It was glutinous and the contents of the tin seemed to be cold.

"What's on TV?" he asked, trying to make conversation.

"You should really try it," said the old man, holding out the can. "It's remarkably good."

He said he was fine, thank you, that he was sorry for barging in like this, all he needed was a few clothes he'd left behind by mistake, he hadn't meant to interrupt.

"I've got to get back to work, you see. At the pub."

"I see," the old man said. "Drop in any time."

THE FAT CRACKS. Faint pops disturb the silent kitchen. In a panic he reduces the heat, dropping the gas right down. He mustn't rush now. The pan can always be made warmer, but if the egg gets too hot too soon then all is lost. He breathes in and out, slowly. A headache gathers behind his brow. No. Focus. Watch the egg. Trails of white start to sketch the egg's circumference, like cirrus across a summer sky. All is well. The fat is under control, the yolk is still whole, the white is slowly cooking. Ever so gently, he turns up the heat, warming the pan incrementally, tilting it to manoeuvre the oil above the flame, allowing small waves to wash around the edges of the egg and brush it gently with heat.

THERE HAD BEEN COMPLAINTS since opening night. Regulars didn't like the new menu. Too fancy, they said.

"It's not fancy," he protested. "It's just good wholesome food."

"It's too fancy," the regulars said. "Where's the burger?"

"Yes," said the landlord, losing patience almost immediately. "Where's the burger?"

"Must there always be a burger on the menu?"

The landlord fiddled with his pen, doodling on an empty work surface. "People like burgers," he said.

He caved to pressure and put a burger on the menu, but he would do it properly. The boys were coaxed into cutting potatoes to make chips and he attempted to teach them to mix relish.

People complained about the relish, said the chips were too big. When they bit into the burger they worried the meat was pink.

"Exactly," he said. "If you cook it through there won't be any flavour."

"Some people don't eat raw meat," the landlord said.

"It's not about being raw or cooked," he said. "Raw and cooked are two sides of the same coin. In a way everything is raw and everything is cooked. The whole thing's a misnomer."

"Some people don't eat raw meat," the landlord repeated.

"Some people are idiots."

Because of the fuss he took the burger off the menu. He refused to serve food that lacked flavour. It went against everything he knew. It went against everything he'd ever understood. He would not kowtow to pressure. People would learn. But they didn't learn. They complained.

"They want the burger back on," the landlord said. "And to be able to choose how it's cooked."

"Do they want to come into the fucking kitchen and cook it themselves?"

"No, they just want their say—it's a matter of taste."

"There are lamb chops on the menu."

"People don't like lamb chops the way they like burgers. It's the bones. It freaks them out having bones on their plate."

He repeated that he was not in the business of sending out food that lacked flavour. People would learn. People would *have to* learn. The previous night he had served two lamb chops, perfectly cooked and rested, to a couple who left most of the meat on the bone and then complained that there was no ice-cream for dessert. After service he drank. He sat at the bar after the landlord had gone home and made the barmaid pour him pints of beer. He drank several as the final guests departed. When the pub shut he told the girl he would lock up and moved on to whisky. He became drunk. Far too drunk. It was not possible for him to drive. He could have, if he'd wanted to; no-one was there to stop him and there were many times in the past when he had, but this time he did not. He slept in his car. When he woke, with limbs that were stiff and a stomach that turned, he knew he had to eat and since he had to eat he figured he might as well cook breakfast, and since he was cooking breakfast he might as well fry an egg.

AT FIRST he saw the old man so rarely that the changes in his diet were hard to notice. Dad would eat at the pub once a week, never poking his head into the kitchen but taking his meals alone by the front window. They didn't speak. They didn't even make eye contact. Instead he gauged the old man's opinion through the debris that was left on the plate. He was delighted when he saw bones licked clean, sauce spooned clear, crumbs of sweet pastry absent. Then one day, a few months after he first found him with the tin of soup in his living room, the old man's weekly order came in: one burger, well done.

"There must be some mistake," he said.

The waitress was despatched to double-check but returned with the same request.

"He's trying to mess with our heads. It's all some sick game. Go back out there and find out what he *really* wants."

The waitress refused.

"There's no way *he* wants a burger."

"Some people like burgers!" the landlord screamed. "And they like them *well done!*"

"Not him," he said.

He charged from the kitchen, soiled whites in tow. The old man was sat up by the window.

"Hello," Dad said with a smile.

"Is this a joke?" he snapped.

"You know," Dad said, "the food here used to be terrible, but it's got a lot better this year."

His eyes burned. It was a setup. There was a game afoot and soon the old man's fury would be launched across the bar and into the kitchen. He sent out the burger, cooked to oblivion: first the oven then the grill. The plate returned. Every scrap was gone. Not so much as a drop of relish left inside the ramekin.

"What did he say?" he demanded of the waitress. "Did he make a complaint? Did he not leave a tip?"

"He said thank you," the waitress said, sucking her teeth, "and that he'd be back next week."

THE YOLK IS RISING SLIGHTLY, so slightly as to be indiscernible, but just enough to suggest that the egg will soon be done. All he needs do is wait for the white to fully settle and then the egg will be cooked. "Every egg that leaves my kitchen looks like this," that French chef had told him. "Every single one."

IT WOULD NOT DO. He was done with the old man's games. After service he left the kitchen and tore round to the house, determined to find out what he was up to. They were adults now. Had been for years, truth be told. They were both too old to be playing games. He found the old man in the lounge, eating cheesy nachos from a large bag.

"Why are you eating fucking crisps?"

The old man paused, a crisp hovering halfway between the packet and his open mouth. He seemed completely taken aback. Eventually, though, he spoke. "Do you want to see the garden?" he said.

The old man led him outside. It had been maybe twenty years since he'd set foot in the garden. He saw the lawn where he'd been told off for skidding his bike and the shed where he'd once been found hammering nails into a can of deodorant. He used to smoke behind the greenhouse until the old man caught him. It was the scene of many punishments. Weekends of forced labour in recompense for his sins. The flowerbed he'd once mown with the lawnmower had long since re-grown.

Perhaps because it had been so long, the old man seemed to think he had to give a whole tour.

"Next spring," he said. "I will plant marigolds here. They do so much better if they get the afternoon sun."

He realised the old man was grinning at him but found himself less and less sure of the joke.

"Do you have time for a glass of orange squash?"

"Squash?"

The old man was already bundling off to the kitchen to measure out two inches of syrup. They sat in the lounge and drank sickly squash. His mind whirled as the old man picked crumbs from the bottom of his packet of crisps.

"Doc told me to cut back on alcohol," the old man said lifting his glass. "But I find these juices are just as refreshing."

The liquid was grainy from where it had been overfilled with syrup. He drained his glass and said he had to get back to work.

"So soon?" the old man said. "There's so much to see in the garden. Will you come again next week? Perhaps we can inspect the flowers then?"

The visits became weekly. Part of a routine. On Tuesday the old man would eat his lunch in the pub and on Thursday, after service, he'd go round to the house for a glass of squash and a tour of the garden.

"Next spring," the old man said, "I will plant marigolds here. They do so much better if they get the afternoon sun."

One time, after the old man had bustled off to retrieve jelly sweets from a bag that seemed to live by his bed, he found a photo album wedged down the side of a chair.

"Ah, yes," the old man said when he returned with the bag of sweets and saw the album open on his lap. "I like those pictures very much. This one is a particular favourite."

On the page was a man, not dissimilar to him, and a boy, not dissimilar to the one he once was. They were seated at a table with knives and forks ahead of them, a joint of gleaming beef in the centre, vegetables steaming beyond.

HE INCREASES THE TEMPERATURE ever so slightly, nudging the egg onwards. It is starting to lift now, to rise above the fat, and as long as he doesn't mess with the temperature it need never descend. At the right temperature the egg can sit there perfectly cooked, ready for when it is needed. He hears a door open, but it can't be the boy as he always comes in through the back entrance. Most likely it's the landlord, armed with his questions about burgers and ice-cream and whisky.

TWO DAYS EARLIER, the old man hadn't shown up for his weekly lunch.

"Are you sure he didn't come by?" he begged the waitress.

She pursed her lips, shook her head. "He did not."

He left the kitchen and walked down the street. He found the old man in his garden, lifting marigolds from the ground and planting them in a tray.

"I have to move these ones," he said. "They're not getting nearly enough sun."

He watched the old man's fingers, thick with sludgy mud, dragging the miniature flowers from the earth. He remembered the day he'd mown them, how the orange petals had shredded until they looked like confetti strewn across the flowerbeds. That day the old man was fury incarnate; today he seemed happy, content.

"Will you pass me that trowel?" the old man said.

"Dad," he said, "have you had anything to eat?"

"Is it that time already?"

The old man's fridge was full of crap: tins of soup, readymade lasagne, crisps, chocolate bars, a family-size bottle of Coke. One shelf was given over entirely to pre-sliced cheese; another to mini sausage rolls. The only thing not processed was a carton of eggs. The old man was already pouring out generous glasses of squash and shuffling off to sit by the television.

He grabbed a pan, filled it with oil and fried an egg.

He worried that the old man would ask for it over-easy or say he preferred it fried to a crisp. Perhaps he now disliked eggs altogether and would rather live on coca cola and crisps. He didn't. He ate the egg greedily. He cut lengths of brilliant white and dipped them into the runny yolk. He chewed and swallowed. He licked his lips.

"I have to get back to work," he said when the old man was done eating and the plates had been cleared away. "But I can come again tomorrow, if you like."

"You know," said the old man, "sometimes I'm not sure I know who you are, but that's one of the best eggs I've ever tasted."

THE BOY HAS ARRIVED, whichever one it is, and is already moaning about the dirty pans in the sink and the mountain of potatoes to peel. He ignores him. The landlord appears soon after and stands behind him in the kitchen. He sounds cross. The pub wasn't properly locked up and there's an empty bottle of whisky on the bar. The landlord wants answers. There are no bookings for tonight and none for tomorrow either. "It's the menu," the landlord says. "It has to change. Things have to change. Do you hear me? Something has to change?"

Beside the stove he adjusts the gas. The egg is done now; perfectly cooked and ready to be put on a plate. But he'll keep it there a little longer; just a little longer; holding it for as long as he can.

Red Sky at Night

I.

PAUL ARRIVES IN PATRAS and lights a cigarette. It is four pm and hot. Sweltering in fact. It has been all summer and even though it is now September the heat shows no sign of letting up. From the coach across southern Greece, Paul had seen trees blackened by forest fires and white walls stained with smoke. He crossed rivers that had become beige dried-up banks and he watched a dog limp across a road to beg an old man for water. Everywhere you look there are signs of the damage being done to the land by the heat, but here in Patras no-one seems to care. Paul finds himself stood by a small park. Old men sit in the shade of cypresses to drink cans of beer; a game of football plays out on a stretch of brown grass; a group of teenage girls huddle around an empty fountain to show each other things on their phones. A young couple pick their way through the crowd with a pram. Above the pram is an elaborate awning presumably designed to protect the infant from the heat. There is no indication as to whether it works. Possibly the child is already dead.

Paul has travelled to Patras from Spetses, where he spent the weekend. He was there to attend a wedding, a friend having decided that it made more sense to get married on a small island in Greece as opposed to say London where Paul and most of the other guests lived. "Perhaps the bride is Greek," Paul's wife, Helen, had suggested when the invitation arrived. "Or maybe her family?" But no, the bride lived in Camberwell and her family came mostly from Gloucestershire, while the groom and his family were Welsh. Yet instead of getting married in London or Gloucester or even Neath, everyone boarded planes and flew to Greece and made their way to the island in the sweltering heat. No-one at the wedding seemed particularly worried about the high temperatures either, but no-one at the wedding seemed particularly worried about anything at all. Over two days Paul didn't think he'd lifted a finger except to raise a glass to his lips or a fork to his mouth. Guests were ferried everywhere by taxi. Iced drinks were widely available. The ceremony was on a clifftop above an olive grove and as the couple exchanged their vows the sun slipped down slowly towards the horizon so that shortly after they were declared man and wife it sunk into the docile sea. Paul thought the whole thing was in poor taste. It was hardly a good omen to have the sun looming over a marriage from the off, not when it was in the midst of battering the earth into submission.

In Patras, Paul's throat rasps. He is painfully dehydrated and, less than twenty-four hours on from the wedding, likely still hungover. He has no interest in the girls and their phones or the football or the old men sat drinking in the shade or even the young couple and their dead child. All he is going to do in Patras is find a taxi that will take him to the port where he has a ferry booked to take him across the Ionian Sea. Paul is due to arrive in Bari early the following morning, giving him time for an espresso and a sandwich before he takes a train north to Milan. In Milan he'll have a couple of hours to eat dinner before the overnight sleeper leaves for Paris, from where Paul will finally take the Eurostar home. Earlier that morning, as the other guests were ferried to the airport, Paul explained to the taxi driver that no, he didn't want to go Athens and could he please be dropped off in Corinth. From there he took a train west. At Kiato the train stopped and Paul found he had to get on a coach because the western section of the Peloponnese railway system had been suspended in 2011 thanks to the Greek austerity programme. This meant that rather than trundling into Patras unimpeded the coach sat sweating in traffic on the outskirts of the city, leaving Paul with barely an hour now until his ferry sails. Paul thus does not have time to see Patras even if he wanted to, but that doesn't matter because the point of the journey home is not sightseeing. No, as Paul explained to the taxi driver, the point of the journey is to experience the distance between things. "The world is very small," Paul said. "Too small in fact. It took two months for the Pilgrims to cross the Atlantic in the Mayflower now you can be in New York in a matter of hours." "What's that got to do with you going to Patras?" the taxi driver asked, mopping his brow with a paper napkin. "My point is that the world is very small," Paul replied. "I want to remind myself how big it is. Also flying is bad for the environment." The taxi driver shrugged, said there was nothing to see in Patras, but that if he was desperate to go there he would drop Paul in Corinth for an extra twenty euros. Paul slept on the train, which was air con- ditioned, but woke up for the coach, which was not. Before they reached Patras they hit gridlock. Bored, Paul flicked on data roam- ing and read the news. There was a flood in Pakistan and a summit in Brazil. By the time the coach stopped, Paul was reading about Patras on TripAdvisor. There really wasn't much to see, a few restaurants with poor reviews and some half-ruined castle on a clifftop. No matter. Paul needs to get moving if he is to catch his boat. He stubs out his cigarette and starts to look for a taxi, but before he reaches the roadside, his phone buzzes in his pocket. As he opens the email he reminds himself to switch off data roam- ing after he's read the message. The last thing he wants is to get home to find a hefty bill all because he was reading about Patras and its stupid castle. Paul squints in the sunlight, rucksack already clammy against his back, and starts to read.

The First Email

From: Helpdesk

To: paulaswell@gmail.com

Subject: Ref. 495856263 URGENT INFORMATION !!!!

PNO NATIONAL SEAMEN'S STRIKE 03rd SEPTEMBER 2018

Dear sir / madam

We regret to inform you that due to the announced PNO National Seman's strike on 03rd September, the departure 03/09 from Patra – Bari will not operate.

Please confirm receipt of this email.

We thank you in advance and we apologize for any inconvenience caused.

Best regards

XXX XXXX

Help Desk

ANEK-SUPERFAST

Lysikratous 1-7 & Evripidou

176 74 Kallithea, Greece

Phone +030 21089 19888

Fax +030 210891988

II.

PAUL STANDS ON THE EDGE of the park and swears. "Fuck's sake," he says. Instinctively he reaches for another cigarette. He hasn't smoked properly for several years because it kills you and so is bad to do. As a younger man he smoked a lot, but by his thirties he was cutting back. For a long time he only ever smoked at parties and New Year and if he had a *really* bad day at work. Then three years ago—or was it four?—he stopped altogether. Paul can't remember precisely when. All he can remember is that as soon as he landed in Greece and felt the heat across his back he marched to a kiosk. He's been chewing through Camel Blues like toffee ever since. He smoked in the hotel bedroom. He smoked by the pool. He smoked through the wedding. He checked with the driver and smoked in the taxi to Corinth. He was not allowed to smoke on the coach, but when they stopped in Diakopto and the driver jumped out Paul leapt out with him and puffed away in the stifling heat. He'd have to stop of course. He's known all weekend that this cannot last. You can't be thirty-six and sit around smoking Camel Blues all day pretending everything will be fine. Paul checks his pack. After the two in the taxi and the one in Diakopto and the one he smoked when he got off the coach and the one Paul lights now there are fifteen left. More than enough to get home if it wasn't for the fucking ferry strike.

"Fuck's sake," Paul says again. This time the young couple look up from the pram. They stare at Paul as if he is some kind of threat. "It's the heat you want to be worried about," Paul says, but the couple ignore him and continue to murmur until Paul leaves. Patras is not a pretty city. It seems tired and unkempt. The streets are dusty and dry. The pavement is missing slabs. Dust clings to every doorstep. Cats and dogs and children scurry through alleyways and on the seafront there is a great deal of litter. It couldn't be more different to Spetses. Paul had arrived on the island in a water taxi that sped across the bay from the mainland. His hotel turned out to be only a short walk through the quiet streets and when Paul was shown to his room he found a view from the window that looked over the town and across the sea to the foothills of the mountains beyond. Paul could see the strange black lines on the mainland, dark streaks stretched out across the hillside that marked the damage done by the fires that had raged across Greece that summer.

When the invitation arrived earlier in the year, Helen had explained that she wouldn't be able to fly out so late in her pregnancy, but as Paul fumed about the distance and the extravagance and the inconvenience she'd reminded him that the bride and groom were his friends why didn't he just go alone. When Paul had flippantly suggested a return journey overland, Helen shrugged and said he should do whatever he thought best. "Makes no difference to me," she said. "I'll stay with my parents." Paul booked a flight to Athens then spent several hundred pounds on a ferry and three train tickets. He felt marginally better about the whole thing. By August, as the wedding fast approached, the heat was starting to disturb the fabric of their one-bed flat: window casements creaked in the night, paint began to peel from the walls. "Maybe they'll have to call the whole thing off," Paul suggested, "because of all these fires?" Helen nodded. She was cutting a banana, smearing it with peanut butter. "Are you not worried about the fires?" Paul asked. "Of course," she said. "But you'll be okay. It's on an island, isn't it?" She laughed at her joke and set about devouring her snack. Paul sulked. He waited for the wedding to be called off, but no, the fires never reached the island. The whole thing would have to go ahead. The day before the wedding Helen got the train to her parents' house and Paul flew to Greece. After he checked into the hotel he left his bag unopened on the bed and went straight to the bar. There weren't many other guests. A couple of families on sun-loungers, an old woman under an awning eating the leftover ice from her Diet Coke. Not long after Paul arrived, a couple came and sat at the table beside him. They spoke English and grinned something silly as they ordered drinks. The man wore a polo shirt and shorts that were trying hard to be chinos. The woman had wrapped herself in a length of fabric and wore sunglasses that covered most of her face. From their conversation, Paul realised they were also in Greece for the wedding. He should probably go over, he thought, and introduce himself, perhaps suggest they all go to the beach or maybe get dinner together that night. The wedding was not until six the following evening so there was plenty of time to get to know each other. When the barman returned, though, and asked Paul if he wanted another beer, Paul shook his head and left. That day he ate lunch by the old harbour staring across at the blackened hillsides and drank more beers than he could strictly afford. What with the train tickets and the ferry booking and the time off work, the trip had cost a lot more than he'd anticipated. In Patras he tries to make amends. At the end of one of the grubby streets he finds the two-star Hotel Byzantino. There is no-one at the reception desk and fifteen minutes pass before a burly man with a ponytail shows up. He appears cross and also strangely wet, as if he'd been sheltering in an ice bath and did not wish to be disturbed. When he realises Paul doesn't speak Greek he hollers into a back room until his daughter emerges to interpret. She is perhaps seventeen, her jaw slack to allow gum to turn between her teeth. It is clear that she hates not only the hotel but also her father. Paul explains that he wants to stay for one night but may need to stay more. He is stuck in Patras, he says, because of the ferry strike and so at this point he doesn't know how long he will be here. As the daughter conveys the message to her father, Paul waits for the man with the ponytail to look up and offer a nod of sympathy, a glance of solidarity, when he recognises that Paul is not some vacant tourist but like him here against his will. The glance never arrives. In desperation Paul asks if the man knows when the strike will end or what the Greek seamen are angry about? His daughter interprets again as the man loads up the hotel computer. His ponytail shakes with his head. He mutters over forms. "He didn't even know there was a strike," his daughter says.

III.

PAUL SITS OUTSIDE a small restaurant that has a TripAdvisor rating of 2.4. Now that it's a little cooler, people have started to emerge from the shadows like soldiers sneaking from bunkers to collect the dead. As the bustle of voices grows around him, Paul lights a cigarette and composes a message to Helen to tell her about the strike. They haven't had a chance to speak properly since the day Paul arrived on Spetses. He called her from the harbour café on his first afternoon as he was drinking all those expensive beers. She asked him about the island and the hotel and whether he'd met anyone yet. "Wedding's tomorrow," Paul said. "Look, I was reading this article on the plane. They reckon when sea levels rise large portions of London could end up underwater." His wife didn't say anything. "Does that not worry you?" Paul said. "Do you think we should move?" "Of course it worries me," she said, "but we don't need to move, we're on the first floor." She laughed and told Paul to relax. "Find some other wedding guests," she said. Paul paid for his beers and walked to a nearby beach where the sand was covered in sun-loungers and music blared from speakers hidden in trees. Paul considers calling her now, but the reception at her parents' place is notoriously suspect and besides he'd only be making another expense. He tells himself he'll call when he has good news and while he waits he orders sausages with tomatoes, green peppers, and spices. By the time his food arrives a cat has come to join him, sat by his feet on the floor. Paul figures that the cat is after scraps from his plate so he saves a piece of sausage and when he has finished, he places the meat on the dirty street. The cat looks at the sausage and then at Paul. A waiter arrives to remove Paul's plate and asks if he'd like another beer. Paul nods and lights another cigarette to go with it. He has thirteen left, which strikes him as unlucky, so when the beer arrives he offers a cigarette to the waiter. The waiter shakes his head. Says he doesn't smoke. Soon after the cat gets up and leaves.

IV.

PAUL WAKES in Hotel Byzantino shortly before seven am. The fan stopped working in the night and the room is already melting around him. In an ashtray beside the bed are two butts from cigarettes that Paul must have smoked before falling asleep. Downstairs the dining area is dotted with fans and guests have clustered around them to eat. The breakfast is formless. Flat bread, wan ham, pale grapes. Paul takes coffee from the stolid urn and flicks through the headlines on his phone. He reads about a government minister who may soon resign, a school in Blackburn without running water, and an elite tennis player who has neglected to pay tax. There is nothing about the heat or the forest fires or the strike by the Greek Seamen's Association. With the second coffee Paul forces down a slice of colourless toast and refreshes his email. He re-reads the message from the Anek-Superfast helpdesk. He lights a cigarette. He sweats. The other guests are also suffering. An old man dabs at his forehead as he fiddles with an apple, a middle-aged couple in loose-fitting clothes sit stock-still beside piles of sliced cheese and dry rolls, and a young woman lifts a tea bag from a cup and waits for it to cool.

On his first morning in Spetses, Paul had also been woken by the sun. Light streamed through the window and he soon gave in, pulled on shorts and sunglasses and staggered downstairs. He found himself sat beside the couple he'd seen the day before. They were called Ruby and Vince and Ruby wondered if Paul was also there for the wedding. Paul saw no point in pretending he wasn't. "It's crazy," Ruby said. "Ben says it's taken over the whole island." "Who's Ben?" Paul asked. Ruby explained that Ben was the guy who worked for the hotel. He was very friendly and gave Ruby and Vince a great tip for a seafood place. Before they could get any further Ben appeared, coming over to the table to check on the guests. Ruby and Vince greeted him with enthusiasm and thanked him for his tip about the fish place. "I had the snapper," Vince said, "barbecued to perfection. You Greeks sure know what to do with your fish." Ben nodded. Smiled. Asked if they were all okay for coffee. Ruby and Vince both asked for fresh cups. Paul, though, was too distracted by the way Vince spoke. The use of the phrase "you Greeks"; the fact that he was doing that English thing of speaking slowly to try and account for non-existent issues in communication. "Yes, *coffee* would be *great*," Vince barked at Ben. The whole thing was embarrassing. When Ben asked Paul if he wanted coffee, Paul shook his head. The sun beat down. A headache percolated behind Paul's brow. Ruby and Vince were still talking. They'd had such a wonderful time by the harbour and met several other guests from the wedding. Soon Ruby was naming people and trying to work out if they had mutual friends. When she mentioned Claire, Paul stopped. "Yes," he said, "she's actually good friends with my wife." Ruby dropped her croissant. Vince rapped the plastic table with his bare knuckles and caused a sugar cube to fall from a bowl. Before Ben returned with their coffees they worked out that Ruby had known Claire and Helen back at university and both she and Vince had declared the world to be very small. No, Paul thought to himself, no, the world is not small at all. In fact it's scarily big. But Paul didn't say any of this. He just nodded and explained that Helen would have liked to be there; she just couldn't travel because she was eight months pregnant. "That's wonderful," Ruby said. "I'm so happy for her, for you both." She grinned across the plastic table. Vince put his hand on her knee. "We've got a little secret of our own," he said. "Ruby's due in the new year." They grinned and started kissing. Oh God, thought Paul, what are we doing? He made his excuses and got up to go back to his room, just as he does after his breakfast in Hotel Byzantino. The ferry office doesn't open until nine. Paul figures he'll take a cold shower to try and stave off the heat then walk over so he's there when it opens. On his way he stops at reception and asks if it will be possible to stay another night. There is a new guy there who has taken one of the fans from the dining room and turned so he can face it directly. "You want to book in for tonight," he says without looking up from the fan. "I don't know yet," says Paul. "It's sixty euros if you want to stay another night," the man says. "I only need to stay if the strike is still going. Do you know if it's likely to carry on into a second day?" "What strike?" the guy says. Paul charges another night to his credit card and returns to his windowless room where he throws himself on the bed. He soon falls asleep.

V.

PAUL VISITS the Anek-Superfast ferry office well after half past ten. There are only two members of staff, a man and a woman, both of them stifling in uniforms that include thick red jackets they seem honour-bound to wear. There is a pitcher of iced water between them and they take it in turns to refill a glass. Paul is determined to let them know that he is aware of how rude and presumptuous English people can be abroad, that he is alive to cultural sensibilities and respectful of local custom and language. He grunts and raises his hand above the height of his shoulder. "Your ferry was cancelled and you want to know when you can leave Patras?" the woman asks. Paul nods. The woman explains that at this point she cannot say. She says the strike is being run by the Greek Seamen's Association, which is nothing to do with Anek-Superfast. The Anek-Superfast crew are not on strike. In fact they are not even allowed to strike. It is in their contracts and besides they are employed by a private company not the state. It is state employees, though, that run the port facilities and it is they who are on strike. "It is very frustrating for us," the woman says. "Until they go back to work none of our ships can leave port." Paul asks when this might be and is told that it is all in the hands of the Greek Seamen's Association. "At this stage we know no more than you," the woman says. "But I know nothing," Paul blurts out. The woman shrugs and reaches for the pitcher of iced water. "Neither do we." Disgruntled, Paul steps outside into the street. He has nine cigarettes left and desperately needs to slow down. Cars speed past and another coach has arrived beside the park to disgorge more passengers into the brutal sun. No-one seems to know how long he will be stuck in Patras, just as no-one seems to know how big or small the world is or what is to be done about all this heat. The sun is remarkably hot today and the city is starting to smell like rotten meat. Possibly there are people dying and festering in the backstreets. Paul wants to find his own corner. Somewhere to curl up and hide.

There was no hiding on Spetses. About an hour after breakfast, Paul was startled by a knock at his door. He found Vince stood in the doorway with a huge grin on his face. He told Paul they should go to the beach. Ruby was tired, he explained, and needed to lie down, which should give the two of them plenty of time to jump on some bikes and explore. Exploring the island was the last thing Paul wanted to do. He'd planned to catch up on sleep and maybe ring Helen later over a pint, but she was going to be tied up with her parents and Vince didn't suggest that Paul had a choice. They hired bikes and cycled through the small town of Dapia past the many beach clubs with their gated entrances and sun-loungers and shades. Vince said there was a more secluded beach beyond the headland, without music rippling from speakers or men in blue polo shirts carrying trays of drinks. Vince's beach was a small cove, empty save for half-a-dozen others who, like them, had sought to escape the hubbub in town. Paul began to feel better. Restored even. As Vince peeled off and dived in the water, Paul lay back on the small angular rocks. At some point he must have dozed off. When he woke Vince was calling his name. Paul walked towards the edge of the water. The sea lapped at his feet. "Are you coming in?" Vince asked. "The sea levels are rising," Paul said. "Are they?" Vince said, walking out of the water. His skin glistened in the bright sun. "Yes," said Paul. "Soon, if they keep rising, thousands of cities will be underwater. Including London. What do you think everyone'll do?" "I expect we'll be all right," Vince said. "We live in Crystal Palace. Come on, there's a rock over there I reckon we could dive off." Paul watched as Vince picked his way along the tideline and clambered over some boulders. He scanned the water carefully, perhaps looking for hazards or trying to gauge depth. "Actually doesn't look so deep from up here," Vince said gingerly. Paul was still stood by the top of the tide. "I wouldn't worry," he said. "Water refracts light, makes it look shallower than it really is." "Oh yeah, I forgot," said Vince. "The water is rising, right?" Vince laughed heartily to himself, then dived in. For a moment his body disappeared beneath the surface and Paul figured he must have been killed, but he quickly re-emerged, his face resplendent with a grin.

VI.

PAUL VISITS Patras Castle, a large triangular ruin from the sixth century, at eleven-fifteen am. No-one else is outside in the midday heat. He walks alone through the city and people stare at him from windows as they shelter in darkened rooms. Steps lead uphill from the city centre and the slope leaves Paul struggling for breath. Sun bleaches his back. His burnt skin winces in the heat. The castle is listed as the city's number one tourist attraction on TripAdvisor and has a rating of 3.5. One of the reviews mentions that during the Byzantine era it was regularly under siege and advancing forces would be repelled by a hail of arrows and rocks. As he climbs Paul thinks about how even the shortest of journeys can become difficult if there are obstacles to cross. This hill, for instance, must add several minutes to the walk and the heat must add even more. He stops to dab his brow with the cuff of his shirt. He thinks of the Byzantine armies who made it up here under a barrage of arrows and rocks.

There were no arrows or rocks in Spetses, but there was a small hill that led through an olive grove to the clifftop where the wedding took place. It was early evening when Paul and Ruby and Vince and the rest of the congregation struggled up that slope. At the reception in the olive grove, Paul found himself telling Vince about a particular type of mosquito that had evolved to live on the London Underground. "I read about that too," Vince said eagerly. "Didn't they say it had already migrated to New York by laying eggs in people's clothes? It's mad how quickly nature adapts." It's not adaptation, Paul thought: we've driven the mosquitos underground. But he didn't say anything, just stood in silence until the waiter came over with champagne. Vince, however, was on a role. As a jazz band started to play he remarked, "Life always seems to find a way." "Are you quoting *Jurassic Park*?" Paul asked. Vince looked confused. "I love that film," Ruby said. Soon they were surrounded by a horde of Jeff Goldblum devotees reeling off quotes, drinking champagne, laughing amidst the olive trees. As he climbs the steps in Patras, Paul fears that an entire generation's perspective on nature might be dictated by a throwaway line in a Hollywood film based on implausible science. No-one is capable of truly believing that life won't find a way despite the myriad daily examples in which life hits a dead end. When Paul reaches the castle, for instance, he finds the gates closed. In desperation he takes out his phone and turns on data roaming to see when it might re-open. He finds that the castle has been under renovation for the last three years and that he has received another email from the Anek-Superfast helpdesk.

The Second Email

From: Helpdesk
To: paulaswell@gmail.com
Subject: EXTENDED: P.N.O. NATIONAL SEAMEN'S STRIKE
03rd – 04th September 2018 --- ADRIATIC SEA SCHEDULES

Good afternoon,

Due to the announced extension of P.N.O National Seamen's strike that will take place on the 4th of September 2018, your reservation has been affected:

(SF 1) Tuesday 04th September 2018
Patras, departure TUE 06:00
Bari, arrival TUE 21:30
<u>WILL NOT OPERATE</u>

Please contact our HelpDesk ANEK-SFF department in order to change your reservation.

We thank you in advance for your consideration and we remain at your disposal for any further assistance you may need.

Best Regards,

XXX XXXX

Help Desk

ANEK-SUPERFAST

Lysikratous 1-7 & Evripidou

176 74 Kallithea, Greece

Phone +030 21089 19888

Fax +030 210891988

VII.

PAUL SLAMS HIS FEET into the steps as he charges downhill. The city is deserted but he marches through the side streets until he finds a bar where the waiter is sat in the shade outside. Paul plonks himself in a chair and barks an order for coffee. He is angry about the castle being closed and the terrible breakfast at Hotel Byzantino and the incessant heat. He needs a salad and a cold drink and to not be in Patras, but instead he drinks the day's fourth coffee and reads and re-reads the email from Anek-Superfast. He reaches into the pack for another cigarette but finds he has only four left. He stops. It is time to be rational. He calls the Superfast number, but it's engaged. He fires off an email to the helpdesk but receives an immediate notification of failure to deliver. There is a text from his phone company to say they're worried about his use of overseas data and another from Helen to say that she did always think the overland journey was a slightly complicated way of coming home. It was your fucking idea, Paul thinks, unsure if that is even true. To celebrate the new stakes of his stay in Patras, Paul orders a beer. He asks the waiter if he knows anything about the strike. "What strike?" says the waiter. "The strike by the Greek Seamen's Association," Paul explains. The waiter shrugs. "People are always on strike," he says. "There's nothing we can do about it. Life has to go on." Paul gulps down the beer and fumes. When did everyone become so convinced that life would persist? Why did no-one in Patras seem to know about the strike and where could he eat a salad? The food at the wedding reception was uniformly rich. Nut purées. Emulsified oils. Rendered fats. Paul drank solidly through-out. First champagne, then white wine, then red. At dinner he escaped Vince and sat next to a man who worked for a pharma-ceutical company. The man told Paul he specialised in expanding markets. "What's an expanding market?" Paul asked. The man explained it was about finding people who were sick but might not yet necessarily know it. When the man began to talk about the opportunities in Africa, Paul excused himself and went to smoke. Later, after the deserts arrived—layers of chocolate and caramel and cream—conversation returned to the sunset they had all wit-nessed as the ceremony drew to a close. Wasn't it beautiful? people said. Wasn't it sensual? Wasn't it just perfect? Someone on the table asked why the sky was so red when the sun set and Paul found himself explaining that the sky turns red when dust becomes trapped in the atmosphere by high pressure; how if the dust particles are small enough they dissipate the blue light leaving only the red rays that give the sky its heartwarming appearance. "But it's not beautiful at all," Paul went on. "Not really, because all that dust has to come from somewhere. All those fires that raged on the coast, the fires that left the hillside blackened and scarred, that's where the dust came from and that's why the sky was so red. So it's not perfect. It's all one big tragic interconnection." There was silence at the table. Guests fiddled with spoons and took long sips from glasses of wine. For a moment it seemed as if the mood had really changed, then from across the table Vince piped up. "But remember guys," he said, "life will find a way." Laughter echoed round the olive grove once more and Paul went off to smoke, tapping ash into one of the many sand buckets that dotted the perimeter of the dining area.

Determined to ration his cigarettes, Paul leaves the dark bar and goes in search of salad. He finds a canteen style café with a TripAdvisor rating of 3.5. It is busy. It is full of people overjoyed to be out of the heat. They lean over one another to take bread from the baskets that dot the tables. There is a counter at the far end and a great fan on the ceiling that controls the temperature. No-one queues. Instead, people call back and forth across the room to two women who deposit plates on the tables. Paul has no idea what the menu says or what words you must shout to cause the women to bring a plate to you. He wavers. Considers going to the McDonald's up the street where you can order on a screen and pay with a card. Before he can leave, though, one of the women marches over and takes him by the arm. She is short and has a firm grip. "Please sit," she says. Paul is placed on a table, brought a beer and a bread basket and a plate of Greek salad. The food is wonderful. Crisp and fresh and light. Afterwards, as she is clearing his plate, the woman asks if he is stuck in Patras because of the ferry strike. "Yes," Paul explains. "Yes, that's why I'm here." She asks where he is going and Paul explains about the overland route. Crossing the Ionian Sea. The trains to Milan and Paris and London. "The world is very small," Paul tells her. "If you just fly everywhere you never really know how big it really is." The woman smiles at him and asks if he would like another beer. When she brings it over she tells him she has never once left Greece. "My sister lived in Paris for a while," she says. "but I never found time to make a visit. I have always been here in Patras. I wake in the morning. I work in the day. In the evenings I go down to the harbour and watch the sunset." Paul nods slowly and lets the effervescent lager still in his mouth.

VIII.

PAUL SITS in the shade of a cypress to drink a beer. It is the hottest, sultriest part of the day and everyone has slowed right down until the sun calms enough for them to move. Paul smokes one of his three remaining cigarettes and wonders what it would be like to be stuck in Patras forever. He rings Helen but she does not pick up. He is meant to remember Ruby to her, to say that once the baby is born Ruby would love to meet up. Ruby had insisted on this when she and Vince said goodbye. By that point the reception had descended into dancing. The tables cleared away. The volume of the music increased. The man who worked in big pharma led a conga line and a girl who claimed to have seen *Jurassic Park* more than twenty times slipped on loose pebbles and grazed her knee. Paul was on his way to the toilets when Ruby came over to find him. They talked about the island and the wedding and the red sunset a few hours earlier. Paul found himself repeating his point about dust and fires and heat but added, "for what that's worth." "Are you okay?" Ruby asked. "Do you want to jump in our cab?" Paul said no he was fine thank you. It was still early, he would stay. "We probably won't see you at breakfast," Vince said, "so give our best to Helen and have a safe flight." As they turned Paul blurted out that he was taking the boat from Patras, he wouldn't be flying home but travelling overland. Ruby and Vince turned. For a moment they both looked terrified, then they forced out smiles. "How exciting," they both said. When Paul eventually made it back to the hotel it was nearly dawn. He stood on the balcony to smoke and stared out across the bay to the blackened hills. In Patras it is now so hot Paul is worried he is going to pass out. The shade from the cypress starts to move and the man sat beside Paul manages to steal it. At one point he leans over and asks Paul for a light. Later, Paul notices another young couple with a pram. The awning is up this time and the baby is gurgling in the bright sunlight. Paul catches their eyes and offers a smile.

IX.

PAUL STROLLS along the harbour wall and smokes his penultimate cigarette. It is a little before eight pm and he stops from time to time to examine the light as it ripples the water. Further along the coast he can see a large ferry with the words Anek-Superfast emblazoned on the side. It is going nowhere and neither is Paul. Instead he sits on the edge of the quay and listens to the sound of kids playing, adults talking, dogs barking. The water ripples with faint lines of light, scattering the evening sun like sparks from a fire's edge. People have clustered at the end of the harbour wall to watch the sunset and a silence gathers on the coast. For a moment all is still as the red globe dips into the gently listing water. The light splits. The water rises. Then at once it is over and everyone moves on. Most people pick up their things to make their way back into town. A scooter speeds past, coughing out fumes, and the couple strolls by once more with the pram. Dogs race along the quayside where Paul sits, waiting until the last of the red light slides from the water and fades away.

The Beach at Oostende on a December evening

HARDLY ANYTHING IS HERE amidst the mist that rises from the tide-line: flecks of salt foam on the quayside; rocks riven ragged by water; air that is thick with sand and high pressure; blue light that does battle with cloud cover; there is a buoy straining out in the channel; an exposed statue; a lone, battered bin; wind that rasps against seawalls and skin; and a voice rising from the boardwalk and calling out a name.

Acknowledgements

I would like to thank the editors of the following magazines where some of the stories in this collection first appeared: *Corda, The White Review, Popshot, Bomb, Structo*, and *Minor Literature[s]*. I am indebted to Daniel Davis Wood and everyone at Splice for conceiving and bringing this collection together. More generally I am grateful to Rebecca Carter for her insight, enthusiasm and guidance. The kindness of many has allowed me to write. Dominic and Andrew have offered reading and reflection, but more importantly friendship. Laura, Duncan and Joe have welcomed me into their family and very often their home. As grandparents, Jilly and Francis and Granny Theo have always showered me with kindness and enthusiasm alike. My siblings, Alice and Henry have long kept me both grounded and entertained, while my parents have been a constant and unwavering source of support. My greatest thanks, though, go to my wife, Holly, without whose love none of this would have been possible.

SPLICE

Lightning Source UK Ltd.
Milton Keynes UK
UKHW011302011219
354565UK00008B/218/P